I GNAWED THE END OF THE QUILL, ABSORBED IN MY LETTER.

"You will not credit this," I wrote, "but Axel's father did not die a natural death at all, and was in fact the victim of a murderous attack last Christmas Eve. It was presumed that the perpetrator was Axel's half-brother Rodric. But he died a few hours after his father as the result of an accident and was unable to defend himself against the charge of murder. Even though it is generally accepted that he was guilty, there are nonetheless those who say ..."

There was a sound behind me. I spun around.

"You should have another candle," said Axel softly, "lest you strain your eyes in such a dim light."

Fawcett Crest Books
by Susan Howatch:

THE DARK SHORE

THE WAITING SANDS

CALL IN THE NIGHT

THE SHROUDED WALLS

THE DEVIL ON LAMMAS NIGHT

PENMARRIC

APRIL'S GRAVE

CASHELMARA

THE RICH ARE DIFFERENT

The Shrouded Walls

by

Susan Howatch

FAWCETT CREST • NEW YORK

THE SHROUDED WALLS

THIS BOOK CONTAINS THE COMPLETE TEXT OF THE
ORIGINAL HARDCOVER EDITION.

Published by Fawcett Crest Books, a unit of
CBS Publications, the Consumer Publishing Division of CBS Inc.,
by arrangement with Stein and Day Publishers

ISBN: 0-449-23385-5

Main Selection of the Bargain Book Club, March, April 1972

Printed in the United States of America

13 12 11 10 9 8 7 6 5

One

WE WERE SEVENTEEN when our parents died. Alexander was away at school in Harrow and I had just begun my last term at Miss Shearing's Academy for Young Ladies in Cheltenham, so neither of us was at home. My father had had an extravagant turn at the Races, drunk too much whisky and then had insisted on taking the reins himself from the coachman and had driven full-tilt across Epsom Downs before misjudging the bend of the road as it sloped to Tattenham Corner. My mother, who was with him, died instantly and my father himself only lived for seven hours afterwards. The tragedy was the talk of society, for our father was a prominent member of Parliament, a gentleman with a country seat in Lancashire and a considerable fortune invested in the cotton mills of Manchester, while our mother was an emigrée from the bloodbaths of the French Revolution, a daughter of an aristocrat whom Robespierre had sent to the guillotine.

Alexander and I did not at first realize we were destitute. It was Sir Charles Stowell, a friend of my father's who finally told us that my father's fortune and estates, including even the town house in London where we had lived all our lives with our mother, had reverted to my father's wife in Manchester. My father had been much too gay and carefree to bother to make a will to provide for his mistress and the twins she had borne him. I could almost hear him saying: "Wills? That's a damned sordid topic of conversation! Who wants to think about death anyway?" And he would have gone on just as before, never once stopping to think that although he himself did not care what happened after his death, there were other people who cared a great deal.

I certainly cared. I cared all the way up to London from Miss Shearing's Academy in Cheltenham, at the inns where we changed horses and stopped to eat, on the rough roads muddy beneath the rain of an English October. I cared when I reached my home, the elegant town house in Soho which my father had bought for my mother's comfort and luxury but never given to her, I cared when I saw the servants whom he had installed to attend our needs, I cared when I saw all the thousand and one other things which now belonged to the middle-aged widow secure in her country home in Lancashire. And most of all I cared when I went to Lincoln's Inn with Alexander to see Sir Charles Stowell and sat in his chambers where the walls were lined with legal books, and the lawns in New Square beyond the window were flaked with autumn leaves.

"But who is to pay for my school fees at Harrow?" said

Alexander blankly to Sir Charles. "I have another year's study to complete there."

"My dear sir," said Sir Charles, who was the smoothest, the most charming and the most realistic of barristers-at-law. "I'm afraid you won't be returning to Harrow."

Alexander still could not grasp the full implications of his predicament. "But I wanted to study at Oxford," he exclaimed hotly. There was a fractious edge to his voice now which I knew and recognized. He had begun to be frightened. "What's to happen to my education?"

"I sympathize," said Sir Charles blandly, "but may I— since we are being so frank with each other—be so discourteous as to remind you that you are fortunate to have received any education at all? Your situation, sir, could be infinitely worse. Fortunately your sister has completed five years at that admirable establishment for young ladies in Cheltenham and will be qualified to seek a position as a governess. As a long-standing friend of your father's I will of course exert what influence I possess to help her obtain employment, but I trust you realize, miss," he added to me, "that your social position is not one which a good family will lightly overlook. However, there are wealthy merchant families who are anxious to employ young females brought up in a ladylike environment, and I dare say something suitable can be arranged. As for you, sir, I can only recommend that you enlist in the army, for you are far too young to be considered as a tutor and you are certainly not qualified to pursue any profession."

"I don't want to enlist in the army," said Alexander. He was white-faced now, very frightened indeed. "I don't want to be a soldier."

Sir Charles looked as if he might say 'Beggars can't be choosers,' but fortunately thought better of it. Instead he gave a regretful little smile, waved his hand in a vague gesture of sympathy and refrained from comment.

"May I ask you a question, Sir Charles?" I said.

"Certainly." He turned his advocate's eyes instantly in my direction. They were very dark and lustrous, and I noticed how his glance seemed to linger on my mouth and the line of my nose before he allowed his eyes to meet mine.

I could almost hear my mother say with contempt: "Men are interested in one thing and one thing only where women such as you or I are concerned. And the more well-bred and righteous the man, the more interested he will be. Let no one fool you."

"How much money do we have now?" I asked him courteously. "This moment, I mean."

"Twenty-five pounds was discovered among your mother's effects; then her jewelry will belong to both of you, and her clothes, and sundry other articles which may be established as gifts from your father to your mother. The house, of course, belongs to Mrs. Cavendish and the responsibility of dismissing and paying the servants will be hers whenever she decides to sell it."

"So in fact we have a little money."

"Enough," agreed Sir Charles, "to keep you until you have found positions for yourselves. That's true."

"Thank you," I said. "And how soon must we leave the house?"

"Mrs. Cavendish has requested that you leave it as soon as possible. Her eldest son—your father's heir—Mr. Michael Cavendish is at present en route to London from Manchester to settle your father's business affairs here. I understand he is to organize the sale of your mother's house."

"I see." My father had talked to us of Michael. "Dull as his mother," he had said, "and twice as pompous." Richard had been his favorite. Richard was the second son. Then there were the four daughters, but they were all older than us as my parents had not met one another until after Mrs. Cavendish's last child had been born. It was strange to think of our half-brothers and half-sisters whom we had never met and even stranger to think of my father having another home in addition to the town house in Soho. He had always seemed to belong to us so completely that the very knowledge that we had always shared him seemed unreal and absurd. Only once had I caught a glimpse of the reality that my mother never forgot, and that was long ago when I was a child and had tip-toed from my bedroom to see them leave the house for an evening at Vauxhall. They had quarreled in the hall in front of the footman. I could still recall the poor footman, his ears pink with embarrassment, as he had stood stiffly by the front door and pretended not to hear my mother cry: "Does it never occur to you that I may be tired of going to Vauxhall and hear all the aristocratic gossip-mongers of London society whisper: 'There goes Mark Cavendish with his blue-blooded French whore?' Does it never occur to you that I might be tired of being ostracized from the circles where I was once accepted and recognized? You—you with your knowledge of London society—is it so impossible for you to visualize how it is to be not just a woman of standing engaged in an indiscreet affair but a man's kept mistress who has borne him two illegitimate children?"

My mother was always bitter. She could remember too

clearly her life in the huge French chateau on the Loire and her brilliant match to the young Duc de Fleury just before the revolution. The London of the turn of the century in which she had found herself widowed and penniless some years later was very different from the world of the *ancien regime* from which she had come. "Emigrés were two a penny," she had told us once, "and if one could not pay the rent the English didn't care how much land one's father had once owned in France. Titles meant nothing at all. Nothing mattered except money, and we were all penniless. How can children like you ever understand? I had never handled money in my life! I was accustomed to ease and riches and luxury, and suddenly I was in a garret in Bloomsbury carrying pitchers of water up six flights of stairs and haggling with the butcher for a cheap portion of beef."

She had started sewing to try to earn money. She had first met Mark Cavendish when she had been altering an evening gown for his wife. Within two weeks she had escaped from the garret in Bloomsbury, the six flights of stairs, the cheap portions of beef. Her one great fear was always losing everything a second time to sink back into the hideousness of poverty, and during the twenty years she spent as my father's mistress she never lost this dreaded feeling of insecurity.

"Anything is better than poverty," she told us again and again. "Anything."

Even being called Mark Cavendish's whore.

"I understand your father," she had said. "I've no illusions about him—or about any other man. I have a pleasant house, sufficient servants, good clothes and my children are well-cared for. Why should I indulge in complaints and regrets? Mark is generous, gay, good-humored and good-looking. What more can a woman expect of a man?"

Kindness, I might have said. Compassion, Understanding. But I said nothing. It was hardly for me to point out that my father was as hard as diamonds, a man who drank hard, gambled hard, rode hard and worked hard. Hard people seldom think of others, not because they deliberately wish to be selfish, but because they are incapable of visualizing anyone else's feelings but their own. My mother might deceive herself because she preferred not to face the truth but I saw all too clearly that for him she was too often a mere convenience, a diversion whom he could always turn to whenever he was tired of his political intrigues at Westminster, his racing at Epsom or his gambling circles in Mayfair.

I never liked him.

Curiously enough I was always the one to whom he seemed the most attached. "Of all my children," he told me once, "I do believe you're the one who's most like me."

Which, considering my opinion of him, I could hardly regard as a compliment.

"Well now, Miss Fleury," said the lawyer, bringing me back abruptly to that book-lined room in Lincoln's Inn with the green lawns outside in the square. "If there are any further ways in which I can assist you, please be so good as to let me know. If you wish for any references while seeking a position as a governess—"

"Thank you, Sir Charles," I said, "but I have no intention of being a governess." I rose to my feet, and the men rose too, Alexander moving the chair so that it would not catch my dress and then assisting me to don my pelisse. "I'm most indebted to you for all your trouble, Sir

Charles," I added to him with my most charming smile. "You've been more than kind."

"My pleasure, Miss Fleury. Please remember that if you should want any further assistance I am always at your disposal." He smiled back into my eyes, making his meaning explicitly clear.

"Thank you," I said. "Good-day."

"Thank you, sir," muttered Alexander, and hurried to open the door for me.

I swept through without a backward glance and outside in the office beyond the little clerk leaped off his stool to open the door which led out into the square.

It was a beautiful day. The sky was blue and cloudless and a light breeze danced through the trees. My mother, who hated English weather, would have said it reminded her of France and the gardens of the chateau on the Loire.

"Oh God," said Alexander desolately.

"Be quiet," I snapped. I was too close to tears myself to stand any nonsense from him. The hired chaise was still waiting at the gates of Lincoln's Inn and presently we were on our way home to Soho.

"What are you going to do?" said Alexander at last.

"I don't know." I stared out of the window at the crowded dirty streets, saw the beggars rattling their alms-bowls and the prostitutes already soliciting in the alleys.

"I don't want to go into the army," said Alexander.

I did not answer.

"Perhaps Michael would help us. After all, he is our half-brother."

I looked at him. He blushed. "I—it was just an idea . . ."

"A very bad one." I went on looking out of the window. "And totally unrealistic."

Presently he said: "You won't have to worry. You'll soon get married, and your problems will be solved. But what about me? How am I to earn a living and support myself? I don't know what to do."

"I should like to know who is going to marry the illegitimate child of an English gentleman and a French emigreé without dowry, portion or social standing," I said acidly. "Please try to talk sense, Alexander, or else don't talk at all."

We traveled the rest of the way home in silence. Soon after we arrived it was time for dinner, and we ate our way wordlessly through the plates of fish, fowl, mutton and beef in the paneled dining room. Above the fireplace our father's portrait smiled down at us, the ironical twist to his mouth seeming a shade more pronounced than usual.

"Perhaps Michael will be here tomorrow," said Alexander.

I was silent.

"Perhaps he will be quite a pleasant fellow."

A clock chimed the hour and was still.

"Perhaps I shall ask him if he can help us."

"If you say perhaps once more, Alexander—" I began and then stopped as the footman came in.

"Yes, what is it, John?"

"There is a gentleman here to see you, miss. He gave me a letter for you and his card, and I showed him into the library."

I took both card and letter from the salver.

"Michael?" said Alexander at once.

"No, it's not Michael." I stared at the card. The name was unfamiliar to me. "I have never heard of this gentleman, John."

"Perhaps the letter, miss—"

"Nor am I in the habit of entertaining strangers known only to me through a letter of introduction."

"Let me see him," said Alexander, standing up. "I'll find out what he wants. Perhaps he's a creditor."

"Pardon, sir," said the footman scandalized, "but he was most definitely a gentleman."

"Nonetheless—"

"Wait," I said. I had opened the letter. The address was New Square, Lincoln's Inn, and the signature at the foot of the page belonged to the lawyer, Sir Charles Stowell. "My dear Miss Fleury," Sir Charles had written. "I hope you will forgive me for taking the liberty to introduce to you by means of this letter an esteemed client of mine, Mr. Axel Brandson. Mr. Brandson, though resident in Vienna, has visited this country many times and as well as being well known to me personally was also slightly acquainted with your father whom he had met during a prior visit to London. On hearing of your bereavement, Mr. Brandson expressed anxiety to offer his condolences and as I was mindful of your present unfortunate predicament it occurred to me that it might perhaps be beneficial if an opportunity could be arranged for him to meet you. I offered to act as intermediary in this respect but Mr. Brandson is hard-pressed by business commitments and it was impossible for us to arrange a suitable time at an early date. Hence I hope that this letter will serve as sufficient introduction to his social position and personal integrity. I remain, etc . . ."

I looked up. The footman was still waiting. "Kindly inform Mr. Brandson, John," I said, "that I will see him shortly, if he would be so kind as to wait a few minutes."

"Yes, miss," said the footman, and withdrew.

"Who is it?" said Alexander immediately.

I gave him the letter.

"But what does he want?" he said mystified when he had finished reading. "I don't understand."

But I was remembering the expression in Sir Charles' dark eyes and the knowledge he had of my predicament and background, and thought I understood all too well. I rose to my feet, trying not to be angry. Sir Charles probably intended well enough. After all I had told him directly I had no intention of being a governess and he had no doubt assumed this declaration to be capable of only one possible interpretation. What else could a woman in my position do if she refused to be a governess? She could only marry, and as no man of any standing would want me for a wife, even that course was denied me.

"Are you sure you should see him alone?" Alexander was saying alarmed. "I'd better come with you. The man's a foreigner, after all."

"So was Mama," I reminded him, "and most of her friends. No, I'll see him alone."

"But do you think it's proper?"

"Probably not, but I don't think that matters so much now." I went out into the hall. In spite of myself I was angry and my pride burned within me like a flame no matter how hard I tried to subdue it by the cool persuasiveness of reason. In a moment of rage I wished the devil would swallow up Mr. Brandson, and Sir Charles Stowell too. I was determined not to make the same mistakes my mother had made no matter how many London garrets I had to spend my days in.

I crossed the hall with swift firm steps, turned the han-

dle of the library door and walked into the room with my
head held high, my cheeks burning and my fists clenched
as if for a fight.

"Miss Fleury?" said the man, turning abruptly to face
me. "How do you do."

He was not as I had expected him to be. I had instinctively visualized a blond giant as soon as I had read of his
nordic names, but this man was dark. He had smooth
dark unpowdered hair, and dark eyes which were as
opaque as Sir Charles Stowell's dark eyes were clear and
expressive; whatever thoughts this man had he kept to
himself. He was dressed sombrely but with good taste in a
dark blue coat and plain well-cut breeches; his carefully
folded white cravat was starched to perfection and his
Hessian boots would have satisfied the highest standards
of elegance. He gave no obvious indication of being a
foreigner for his English was flawless, and yet I was at
once aware of some cosmopolitan nuance in his manner
which was difficult to define. When he took my hand and
bowed I noticed that his fingers were long and slim and
cool against my hot palm.

"Pray be seated," I said graciously, withdrawing my
hand rather too quickly. "May I offer you a cordial or
some other refreshment?"

"Thank you, but no." His voice was cool too, I noticed. The lack of accent somehow seemed to take all hint
of passion from his tone.

We sat down by the fireplace, opposite one another,
and I waited for him to begin a conversation.

Presently he said: "You may well be wondering who I
am and why I have effected this introduction to see you. I
must apologize for trespassing on your privacy at such a
distressing time. It was kind of you to see me."

I made a small gesture of acknowledgement.

"Permit me to offer my condolences to you on your bereavement."

"Thank you."

There was a silence. He crossed one leg over the other and leaned back in his chair with his hands tightly clasped in front of him. The light slanted upwards across his cheekbones and into his opaque eyes. "I consider myself Austrian, as I have lived in Austria most of my life, but in fact I am half-Engligh by descent. My father is—was— an Englishman. He died ten months ago."

I wondered if I should comment. Before I could make up my mind he said: "My mother returned to Austria shortly before I was born and died five years afterwards, leaving me both property and income in Vienna. I was more than content to stay there, although I was educated in England and later often came here on account of my business interests; occasionally I would travel down to Sussex to see my father. He remarried soon after my mother's death and had other sons by this time."

He paused. I contrived to look intelligent and attempted to give the impression I knew exactly what he was trying to say.

"My father was a rich man," he said. "He had estates on the Romney Marsh and his ancestors were prominent citizens of the Cinque Ports. I assumed that when he died he would leave his house (which was not entailed) and his wealth to his eldest son by his second marriage, but I was wrong. He willed everything to me. My commitments in Vienna made it impossible for me to come to England earlier, but I am here now for the purpose of visiting the estate and seeing my English relations."

"I see," I said.

"I rather doubt whether you do," he said ironically, "since I haven't yet explained why I have come to see you. However, I appreciate your interest in what to you must seem a very puzzling narrative." His hands were clasped so tightly together that the knuckles gleamed white. He glanced into the fire for a moment and then looked back at me swiftly as if he had hoped to catch me off my guard. Something in his expression made me avert my eyes instinctively and make a great business of flicking a speck of dust from my cuff.

"Pray continue, sir," said my voice politely.

"I happened to visit my lawyer Sir Charles Stowell this morning," he said. "There were one or two matters relating to my father's will that I wanted to discuss with him, rather than with my father's lawyers in Rye. In the course of conversation Stowell mentioned your name and the— circumstances of your position both before and after your parents' death, as he considered it might be germane to my position."

"And pray, Mr. Brandson," I said so cooly that my manner was even cooler than his, "what is your position?"

"Why, merely this, Miss Fleury," he said, and to my annoyance I sensed that he was amused. "If I wish to inherit under the terms of my father's will, I must marry within one year of his death. Furthermore it's specifically stipulated that my wife must be English by birth. Unfortunately this condition is not nearly so easy to fulfill as it might have seemed to my father when he made his very insular stipulation. To begin with, the ladies of my acquaintance are all Viennese, not English; I know of no eligible young Englishwoman, and even if I did it's possible that her father would frown on my foreign blood and discourage the match. My father, as I am well aware, was not the only insular man in this extraordinarily arrogant country, and now when England is the richest, most powerful nation in the world she is more insular and arrogant than ever before. On the other hand, it was clear to me that I couldn't merely marry some serving-girl for the purpose of fulfilling the condition in the will. My wife must know how to conduct herself and be at ease among people of the class with whom I would be obliged to associate on accepting the inheritance. She must at any rate give the appearance of poise and breeding."

My coolness seemed to have turned to ice. I was unable to move or speak. All I was conscious of thinking was: He wishes me to masquerade as his wife. When he has his inheritance safely in his hands I shall be discarded and left penniless.

"I believe you are seventeen years of age, Miss Fleury," he said. "I assume that by this time you will have considered the idea of marriage in general terms, if not in relation to any specific person."

"Yes," I heard myself say. "I have considered it."

"And?"

"And put the thought aside."

"May I ask why?"

"Because," I said, trying to erase all trace of anger from my voice, "I have no dowry, no portion and no social standing. The possibility of making a good match is out of the question."

"I think you underestimate your own attractions," he said. "Or else you overestimate the disadvantage of your background. I am sure you would have no difficulty in finding suitors."

"It's plain to see you're a foreigner, Mr. Brandson," I

said, my tongue sharp in my desire to stab back at him for his casual reference to my illegitimacy. "If you knew this country better you would know that whatever proposals a woman such as I may receive, none of them would have anything to do with matrimony."

"But I have just proposed matrimony to you," he said undisturbed. "Am I to understand that my proposal was not worthy of your consideration? You at least cannot reject me as a foreigner, Miss Fleury! My father was as English as your father was, and your mother was as much a foreigner as mine. My reputation and standing both in London and Vienna are excellent—anyone will confirm that. I have no title, but my father's family fought with Harold at Hastings against the Conqueror and my father was one of the most respected of the landed gentry throughout the length and breadth of Sussex. If you married me you would find yourself the wife of a prosperous land-owner, mistress of a large and beautiful home with plenty of servants."

After a while I said: "You want to marry me?"

For the first time since I had met him he smiled. "I am only surprised that you should find it so hard to believe," was all he said.

"A legal binding marriage?"

"Certainly. An illegal fraud would be of little use to me in making any claim to the estate, and still less use to you."

My incredulity was succeeded by an exhilaration which in turn sharpened into panic. "I—we know nothing of each other—"

"What of that? The majority of marriages these days among people such as ourselves are preceded by a very brief acquaintance. Marriage is an institution of convenience which should confer benefits on both parties. The grand passion of a courtship culminating in married bliss is for operatic librettos and the novels of Mrs. Radclyffe."

"Well, of course," I said sharply, not wanting to be thought a romantic schoolgirl, "it was not my intention to imply otherwise. But—"

"Well?"

"I—I don't even know how old you are!" I cried out. "I know nothing of you!"

"I am thirty-four years old," he said easily. "I was married in my twenties, but my wife died in childbirth and the baby with her. I've never remarried." He stood up. "You will of course need to consider the matter. If you will permit me, I shall wait upon you tomorrow, and then if you wish to accept my proposal we will take a drive in the park and perhaps drink chocolate in Piccadilly while we discuss the plans further."

"Thank you," I said. "I assume you have no objections to my brother accompanying me? I would prefer to be chaperoned."

He hesitated slightly, and then shrugged his shoulders. "As you wish."

"Before you go," I said, for he was still standing, "I would like to clarify one or two matters in my mind."

"Certainly." He sat down again and crossed one leg over the other. His hands were no longer clasped tightly together, I noticed, but were limp and relaxed again upon his thighs.

"First," I said, "if I am to marry you, I would like to be sure that my brother is provided for. He has another year of studies at Harrow and then would like to go up to Oxford to complete his education."

"That could easily be arranged."

"And he could have a reasonable allowance and live under our roof whenever he wishes?"

"By all means."

"I see," I said. "Thank you."

"Was there some other matter you wished to clarify, Miss Fleury?"

"Yes," I said. "There was." My hands were the ones which were clasped tightly now. By an effort of will I held my head erect and looked him straight in the eyes. "There's one matter on which I'm anxious there should be no misunderstanding."

"And that is?"

"As the marriage is really purely for convenience, Mr. Brandson, am I to take it that the marriage will be in name only?"

There was a silence. It was impossible to know what he was thinking. Presently he smiled. "For a young girl educated in an exemplary seminary for young ladies," he said, "you seem to be remarkably well-informed, Miss Fleury."

I waited for him to speak further but he said nothing more. After a moment I was obliged to say: "You haven't answered my question, sir."

"Nor have you commented on my observation, madam."

"That's easily done," I said shortly. "My mother talked long and often of marriage and liaison and of the lot of women in general."

"In that case," he said, "you will be well aware that there are few marriages which begin in name only although the majority certainly end in that manner. However, if the matter is distasteful to you, there is no need for us to live together immediately. As you say, I am more interested in securing my inheritance and you are more interested in attaining your own security to be concerned with details such as those. We can discuss them later on."

My first thought was: He thinks I am as fearful as most young girls and might spoil his plans by refusing in panic at the last minute to marry him. My second thought: He has a mistress or he would not concede so much so carelessly.

And my relief was mingled with anger and irritation.

"Then I shall see you tomorrow?" he said, rising once more to his feet. "If I may, I would like to wait upon you at half-past ten tomorrow morning."

"Thank you," I said. "That would be convenient."

He took my hand again in his long cool fingers and raised it casually to his lips. I felt nothing at all. No shiver of excitement or anticipation or even revulsion. He merely seemed old to me, a stranger twice my age with whom I had nothing whatever in common, and it was at that time quite impossible for me to realize that within a month we would be sharing the same name.

"But we know nothing of him," said Alexander. "Nothing. We don't even know that he is as he says he is. He may be utterly disreputable."

"We shall go now and talk to Sir Charles Stowell. Tell John to have the chaise brought to the front door."

"But an Austrian! Viennese!"

"Austria is allied with us now against Bonaparte."

"But—"

"Listen Alexander. Please try to be practical and realistic. We're not in a position to be otherwise. Within a few days we shall be destitute—we have no money and soon we'll have no roof over our heads either. This man—if he is as he says he is, and I believe he was telling the truth—this man is going to provide us both with financial security and social respectability. It's a gift from the gods! I shall be an honorably married woman with a house and servants, and you will be able to complete your studies and then do whatever you wish. How can we turn down such an opportunity? What shall we do if we did turn it down? You would have to enlist in the army and I should have to be a governess, and while you may be content to spend the rest of your life marching and parading, *I* am not content to be consigned to some isolated country mansion to teach the stupid children of some provincial local squire! I want to marry and be a great lady in whatever county I may live in, not to be a spinster, an unwanted appendage to a noble household!"

"You would be content to marry this man?"

"You didn't see him!"

"I didn't care for your description of him."

"But Alexander," I said exasperated, "this is hardly the time to be particular and fussy about prospective brothers-in-law, or husbands. Mr. Brandson is not ill-looking, he is courteous and a gentleman, and he cannot help being old. It could be much worse."

"Well, I don't like it," said Alexander obtusely. "I don't like it at all. Who knows what this may lead to?"

"Who knows?" I agreed. "But I know very well what would happen if we ignored this offer. Suit yourself, Alexander, but which is the worse of two evils?"

"I wonder," said Alexander.

Mr. Brandson arrived punctually at half-past ten the

following morning and I went to the library to greet him
with my decision. I was wearing a dress of yellow muslin
in the height of fashion, and my maid had arranged my
hair in a most becoming Grecian style so that I considered myself exceptionally elegant. My self-confidence
swept me across the floor towards him and only ebbed
when I felt his cool fingers once more against my hand.
There was some element in his manner which unnerved
me. For the first time it occurred to me that he was sophisticated; he was probably amused at my attempt to
present an adult poised facade to him, much as any mature man would be amused at the caprices of a precocious
child.

With singular lack of finesse I managed to say gauchely
that I had decided to accept his proposal.

It seemed that he had never once thought that I would
do otherwise. He had all his plans carefully prepared. He
had rented a suite of rooms near Leicester Square, he
said. He understood the predicament in which my brother
and I were placed, and suggested we might move to the
rooms whenever it became necessary for us to do so. I
might take my maid with me, if I wished. He and I could
be married as soon as was convenient and could spend a
few days in the country after the wedding while Alexander could return to Harrow.

I said that this would be eminently satisfactory.

News of my betrothal was soon circulated; my mother's
French friends who eventually came forward to offer us
assistance were all relieved to hear that I had been so
fortunate although little was known of Mr. Brandson.
However, one or two people had heard of his father
Robert Brandson, the Sussex land-owner, and Sir Charles

Stowell introduced me to a City banker who assured me of Mr. Axel Brandson's standing as a man of business in London and Vienna.

Mr. Brandson himself gave me a handsome sapphire ring and waited on me five out of the seven days of each week. Often he stayed no longer than quarter of an hour before making some excuse to be on his way, but occasionally we went for a drive in his phaeton, and once, shortly before the wedding he took me to Vauxhall.

I was unchaperoned. Now that I was officially betrothed and soon to be married it was no longer so important to be escorted by a third person, and besides Alexander had an assignation with some actress with whom he had become infatuated during frequent visits to the theater in the Haymarket, and I saw no reason to interrupt his schoolboy's idolization of some highly unsuitable female. The worst that could happen would be for her to be too indulgent towards him.

So I went to the pleasure gardens of Vauxhall with Axel Brandson and walked with him among the brilliantly-dressed crowds. I was just enjoying being seen in the company of my future husband by people I knew, and was just lagging a pace behind him to make sure that I had not mistaken some fashionable member of the aristocracy nearby when I heard a man's voice exclaim: "So you're back, Axel! And alone! What happened to the beautiful—"

I turned. The man saw me and stopped. There was a second's silence and then Mr. Brandson said without inflection: "Miss Fleury, allow me to present an acquaintance of mine . . ."

But I was not listening to him. The man's name was

familiar to me. My father had spoken of him in vague amusement as "a daredevil rake and a gambler soaked in his own debts." Since my father was a rake and a gambler I knew exactly the kind of man Mr. Brandson's friend was.

"You told me you had no friends in London," I said after we had left the gentleman behind.

"No close friends certainly."

"The gentleman seemed very well acquainted with you."

"Once perhaps fifteen years ago we were inseparable during my visits to England but that time is long since past." He seemed untroubled, but I thought I could detect a slight impatience in his manner as if he wished to be rid of the subject. "My personal friends are in Austria now. The people I knew in London are merely business acquaintances."

"And the beautiful lady he referred to? Is she also a mere business acquaintance?"

He gave me such a long cool look that in the end I was the first to look away.

"I have been a widower ten years, Miss Fleury," he said at last, and his voice was as cool as his expression. "As you are already so well acquainted with the ways of the world you will be well aware that once a man has become accustomed to female companionship he is loth to do without it later on. Shall we turn here and walk in another direction, or do you wish to go home yet?"

Tears pricked beneath my eyelids for some reason not easy to explain. I felt very young suddenly, and, what was worse, insecure and afraid. At that moment my betrothal seemed no longer a fortunate stroke of luck, a game which enabled me to parade among society at Vauxhall and display my future husband, but an exchange of freedom for restriction, of the familiar for the unknown.

It made no difference that I had already guessed he must have a mistress. The casual way he had not even bothered to deny the fact and his mockery of my desire to appear sophisticated were the aspects of his behavior which I found most hurtful. When I reached home at last I went straight to bed and tossed and turned with my tears till dawn.

The next morning he called with an enormous bouquet of flowers and was at his most courteous and charming. Even so I could not help wondering whether he had spent the night alone or whether he had visited his mistress instead.

We were married in the church of St. Mary-le-Strand less than a month after we had met and Alexander and Sir Charles Stowell acted as witnesses. It was a very quiet affair. My French godmother, an old friend of my mother's, attended, and two or three of my childhood friends. Afterwards there was a wedding breakfast at my husband's rented townhouse, and after it was over the carriage was waiting at the door to take us the twenty miles south into Surrey to the country house where it had been arranged that we should stay for a few days. The owner, an acquaintance of Axel's was at that time in Bath with his family, and had given instructions that we were to treat the house as if it were our own.

My traveling habit consisted of a fur-trimmed redingote of levantine worn over a classic white muslin dress, and accompanied by a matching fur muff and snug warm boots to combat the chill of November. Axel had given me plenty of money so that I could have the clothes I pleased for the wedding and afterwards, and although time had been short I now had an adequate wardrobe for the occasion.

"You look very fine," said Alexander almost shyly as he came forward to say goodbye to me. And then as he embraced me I could hear the anxiety in his voice as he said uncertainly: "You will write, won't you? You won't forget?"

"Of course I shan't forget!" There was a lump in my throat. Suddenly I couldn't bear to leave him, and hugged him fiercely to me with all my strength.

"I shall see you at Christmas," he said, "when I am able to leave school for the holidays."

"Yes."

"It won't be long. Just a few weeks."

"Yes." I disengaged myself and turned away before he could see how close I was to tears.

"You will be all right, won't you?" he whispered as I turned from him.

"Of course!" I said with dignity, recognizing his craving for reassurance and not daring to acknowledge my own. "Why not?"

Axel was waiting a few paces away by the carriage. He had already said goodbye to Alexander. As I could sense they both disliked each other, I wasn't surprised that their parting from one another had been very brief and formal.

I reached the carriage.

"You're ready?" said Axel.

"Quite ready, thank you."

He assisted me into the carriage and then climbed in after me. It was not until we were well out of London that I was sufficiently in control of myself even to look at my husband, let alone speak to him. Finally as we passed through Wandsworth I was able to say: "How fortunate that the weather should be so fine."

"Yes," he said, "indeed."

I looked at him. His polite expression told me nothing, but I knew instinctively that he was well aware of my emotional battles and had carefully refrained from conversation to avoid giving me embarrassment. I suppose I should have been grateful to him for his perception and consideration, but I was not. I somehow resented the fact that he saw too much and understood too well, and I was angry.

We stopped at Epsom where we dined, and again at Leatherhead where we paused at the inn by the river to allow the grooms to attend to the horses. By the time we reached the village of Bookham and the mansion of Claybury Park it was dusk and I was feeling very tired.

The house seemed spacious and beautiful, even to my weary eyes, and the servants civil and attentive. Axel asked if I wanted any refreshment and when I refused told one of the servants to show me to my room.

A fire blazed in the grate and the lamp on the table illuminated the gracious furniture of a room of elegance and style. After glancing around with interest, I locked the door into the corridor and went over to examine another door on the far side of the room. As I suspected it led into another bedroom where Axel's luggage had already been placed by his valet. After glancing at the heavy portmanteau, I closed the door and looked for the key to lock that as well, but there was no key to be seen.

I decided not to summon my maid. She would be as tired as I was, and I could manage well enough on my own. Undressing as quickly as I was able, I loosened my hair, brushed it out and dowsed the lamp. The flames still flickered in the grate and I lay awake a long time watching them and listening for any hint of Axel's arrival in the room beyond. Time passed. My eyelids grew heavy and my thoughts became more detached. I thought fleetingly and without distaste of my brief acquaintance with Axel Brandson and the quiet unobtrusive wedding. I still could not entirely believe that I was a married woman and that Axel was my husband. It was a pity he was so old and seemed to have so little to say to me. It was true he was courteous and often charming but I had always had the impression that he was making an effort to appear so. I probably seemed a mere child to him, and he had been bored.

I wondered what his mistress was like, and was suddenly determined to outshine her. "He shall not be bored by me!" I thought furiously. "He shall not!" I hazily began to imagine passionate love scenes throbbing with romance and tenderness, a state of ecstasy unrivaled by anything I had ever experienced before. After all, as I reasoned, such a state must be enjoyable or people would not spend so much time thinking of so little else.

My eyes closed. I was warm and luxuriously comfortable. I was just about to drift into sleep when I thought of Alexander and wondered if he was thinking of me.

The loneliness hit me in a hideous wave, driving away the comforting oblivion of sleep and making my throat ache with the longing to cry. I stared for a long time at the dying embers in the grate, and then at last I heard movements from Axel's room and I was conscious of an enormous relief. My pride alone restrained me from running to him in my desire to shut out the loneliness and seek comfort from the only person I could now turn to.

I waited. Gradually the sounds ceased and there was

silence. I went on waiting, my limbs stiff with tension, but he did not come. I waited until the fire had died in the grate and then I turned and buried my face in my pillow and wept myself to sleep.

The next morning it was raining. My maid, Marie-Claire, helped me dress and arranged my hair but I was disinclined to talk and I could sense she was disappointed. When I was ready I went downstairs, uncertain of my way around this strange mansion, and was directed by a footman to a small breakfast room where I drank a cup of tea and ate a biscuit. Afterwards I wandered through the rooms listlessly and stared at the view from the windows of the long gallery but the rain had brought mist to the valley and it was difficult to see much. I wished that it could have been fine for the grounds looked interesting and it might have been pleasant to wander in them, but it was much too wet to go out.

In the end I went to the library, found one of Jane Austen's novels and tried to read, but the placid events which befell her characters soon bored me and I turned instead to Fielding and Defoe. There was even a copy of *Moll Flanders* which my mother had never let me read, so the morning passed unexpectedly quickly.

I saw nothing of Axel until dinner was served at three. I was very cool towards him, but he seemed not to notice and was as polite—and as remote—as ever. Afterwards I left him alone with his port and went to the drawing room to write a letter to Alexander. I described the house in great detail and told him all about *Moll Flanders*.

I felt better after that.

Presently it was time to go to bed and I took a great deal more trouble with my appearance and wore my best nightgown which weariness had made me ignore the night before. Once in bed I tried to stay awake for as long as possible but sleep claimed me before I was even aware of its approach and when I awoke the night was far advanced and I was still alone.

I think Marie-Claire was a little hurt that I should be so morose and silent for a second morning in succession, but I made no effort to talk to her and eventually she withdrew sulking while I went down to breakfast. Fortunately it was fine and I spent the morning wandering around the grounds, exploring the lawns and yew walks, the vegetable garden and orangery, the woods, the stream, and even the ruined temple which had been erected a generation earlier to ornament the grounds.

Axel spent the morning writing letters. I had gone into the library to return *Moll Flanders* to its shelf and he had already been seated at the desk with pen and ink. We had said good morning to each other and exchanged a few polite words. Later when I returned to the library before dinner to look for another book to read I found that he had gone but the letters lay on the desk where he had left them. I glanced at the addresses. Three were marked for Vienna, but one was addressed to "James Sherman Esquire, Sherman, Shepherd and Sherman, Solicitors, 12 Mermaid Street, Rye, Sussex", and the last to "Vere Brandson Esquire, Haraldsdyke, near Rye, Sussex." I stared at this last letter for some time. Haraldsdyke, I knew, was the name of the estate and house which Axel had inherited from his father, my future home where I would be mistress. Vere Brandson was the second son of Axel's father's second marriage. The eldest son, Rodric, Axel had told me, had died shortly after his father as the result of an accident. The youngest son, a boy of nineteen whom Axel had scarcely referred to at all, was called Edwin.

I was still thinking of Axel's English relations when I went down to dinner and was tempted to ask him more about them, but he seemed disinclined to conversation and apart from inquiring politely how I had spent my day and embarking on a discussion of landscape gardening, he appeared anxious to eat in silence. I was therefore a little surprised when he joined me in the drawing room later and suggested that I played for him on the spinet for a while.

I have never been fond of the spinet but I play passably well and sing better than I play. He seemed pleased at my ability, and as I naturally enjoyed his compliments I offered to play a piece on the harp. There is only one piece I can play well on the harp, and I played it. To my satisfaction he asked me to play more but I pretended to be too modest, and gracefully escaped the risk of spoiling the excellent impression I had created.

"I'm delighted I have such an accomplished wife," he said, and his smile was so charming that he seemed handsome to me for the first time. It was also the first reference he had made to our new legal relationship with one another. "I had no idea that you were so musical."

"There was no spinet in the rooms you rented for Alexander and myself," I said lightly. "I had no chance to play to you before."

"True." He smiled at me again. "You speak French, of course?"

"Yes."

"Perhaps you would read me some Molière if you were not too tired? There's nothing I like better than to hear French spoke with a perfect accent."

I was reminded again of his foreign background. No true Englishman enjoyed listening to the tongue of the great national enemy Bonaparte.

I read to him in French for half an hour. I was perfectly at ease in the language, as my mother and I had always spoken French to one another and I had had a French maid from an early age. Afterwards he again seemed pleased and we talked for a while of French literature and history.

We had a light supper by candlelight at last, and then he said that he was sure I was tired and that if I wished to retire to bed he would quite understand.

I could not decide whether he was being genuinely considerate or whether he merely wished to dismiss me. However, I went upstairs to my room, conscious of a feeling of disappointment, and sat for a long while before my mirror frowning at my reflection in despondency. Finally, trying to stave off my increasing loneliness I summoned Marie-Claire and made an elaborate toilette before preparing myself for the long hours of the night which lay ahead.

I had not been in bed more than ten minutes before I heard movements in Axel's room. There was the faint sound of voices as he dismissed his valet, and then later after more vague sounds there was silence. I was just straining my ears to decide whether or not he had gone to bed, when the communicating door opened and he came into the room.

I half-sat up in my surprise and at the same moment he turned to look at me. The flame flickered on the candlestick in his hand and was reflected in the darkness of his eyes so that their expression was again hidden from me.

I sank back upon the pillows.

For a moment I thought he was going to speak but he did not. He set the candlestick down on the table by the side of the bed and then gently snuffed it out so that we were in darkness. I heard rather than saw him discard his dressing gown; suddenly he was beside me between the sheets and I could feel his quick hot breath against my cheek.

I relaxed happily in the supreme bliss of my ignorance. I had thought myself so sophisticated in knowing all about the passion and ecstasy and fulfillment of the act of love. No one had ever told me that this same act could also be painful, embarrassing and repulsive.

Later after he had gone I curled myself up into a ball as if to ward off the horror of memory, and for the third night in succession I cried myself to sleep.

It was raining again the next morning and I was unable to walk in the grounds. After breakfast I took another of Miss Austen's books from the library and hid myself in the smallest morning room while I read it. Today Miss Austen's work was easy to read, her situations no longer mundane, her characters no longer boring but reassuring in their normality. I no longer wanted to read Gothic romances or any novel such as *Moll Flanders,* and Miss Austen's world of vicarage and village and social proprieties was soothing and comforting to my mind.

Axel found me at noon. He was wearing riding clothes, and I noticed for the first time then that although it was still gray outside the rain had stopped.

"I wondered where you were," he said. "I couldn't find you."

I knew not what to say. Presently he closed the door behind him and crossed the floor slowly to my couch.

"I doubt whether there's much sense in delaying our departure for Haraldsdyke much longer," he said as I fingered the leather binding of the book in my hands. "Today is Saturday. Unless you object, I thought we might leave on Monday morning. If the roads are not too disgraceful we may reach Rye on Wednesday night."

"As you wish."

He was silent. Presently I felt his cool fingers against my cheek, but I did not look up; I was steeling myself against any reference he might make to the distasteful memory which lay between us, but in the end all he said was: "There's no need to look as if you think the company of the opposite sex is a sadly overrated commodity. Matters will improve in time." And then he was gone before I could attempt to reply, and I was alone once more with my book in the silent room.

I wondered when "in time" would be, but evidently it was not to be beneath the roof of Claybury Park. That night and the following night the door between our bedrooms remained closed, and on Monday we left the lonely peace of that beautiful house in Surrey for the mists of the Romney Marsh and the shrouded walls of Haraldsdyke.

Two

"PERHAPS I SHOULD tell you more about my family," Axel said as we dined together on Monday night at Sevenoaks.

Outside it was dark, but where we sat in the private sitting room accorded to us by the innkeeper, a huge fire blazed on the hearth and the room was warm and comfortable. After the tediousness of the long hours of travel it was a relief to escape from the jolting post-chaise and the chill of the damp weather.

"Yes," I said uncertainly, "I would like to hear more about your family. You only described them so briefly before." I was uncertain because I was by no means sure that this was the answer he wanted. At the same time I was also annoyed that I should be so nervous with him that a single chance remark should throw me instantly into a state of confusion.

I began to examine a scrap of roast beef with meticulous care, but when he next spoke he seemed unaware of my embarrassment.

"My father died last Christmas Eve, as I've already told you," he said. "He was a man of strong personality, typical of many an English gentleman who belonged to the last century rather than to this one. He was a staunch Tory, a confirmed conservative, a believer in letting his land be farmed the way it had been farmed since the Conquest, violently anti-Bonaparte and anti-European. It always amazed me that he of all people could have brought himself to marry a foreigner, but maybe he was more liberal when he was younger. Or maybe his experiences with my mother contributed to his later prejudices against foreigners. They certainly weren't happily married. She left him even before I was born, but fortunately had the means to set up an establishment of her own in Vienna where I entered the world a few months afterwards. Following my birth she never fully regained her health and in fact died five years later. After that I was brought up by her elder brother, my uncle, who was later appointed to the Court of St. James's on some minor diplomatic mission in the days when the Emperor was still Holy Roman Emperor, and not merely Emperor of Austria as he is today. I went with him to London, and my uncle, who had always found me rather an intrusion on the privacy and freedom of his bachelor existence, arranged for me to meet my father in the hope that my father would perhaps relieve him of his responsibilities where I was concerned.

"My father came to London—probably more out of curiosity than anything else—to see what his half-foreign son was like. I remember very well when I first saw him.

He was very tall, taller than I am now, and wore a wig which looked as if it had seen better days. He had an enormous paunch, massive shoulders and a voice which I believe would have frightened even Bonaparte himself. I could well understand how he managed to have such powerful influence in the town of Rye and the other Cinque Ports, he would dominate any gathering. England was, and is, the richest, most powerful country in the world, and he was to me then a personification of England—tough, arrogant, self-opinionated and rude—but generous to a fault with his money, compassionate when something touched his heart, and unwaveringly loyal to his friends, to his king and country and to those principles which he believed were right and just.

" 'Ho!' he said, entering the room with steps which made the china tremble on the mantelpiece. 'You look just like your mother! Never mind, you can't help that. What's your name?'

"He nearly expired when I told him. His face went purple and his eyes were bright blue with rage. 'Damned foreign nonsense!' he roared. 'I'll call you George. What's good enough for the king should be good enough for you. What's all that Frenchified nonsense around your throat and wrists?'

"It was the fashion in Vienna at the time for small boys to wear jackets with lace cuffs and a lace kerchief, but my English wasn't good enough to tell him so. 'Zounds!' he said (or something equally old-fashioned), 'the child can't even speak his native tongue! Never mind, my boy, we'll soon put that right.'

"So he promptly removed me from my uncle's care, much to my uncle's relief, took me to Haraldsdyke and hired a tutor to teach me English. He had married again by this time, but my half-brothers Rodric and Vere were little more than babies and Ned was yet to be born, so I was a solitary child. When I was twelve he sent me off to Westminster in the hope that boarding school would complete the process of turning me into a young English gentleman.

"I left there ignorant but tough at the age of eighteen and asked to go back to Vienna as I suspected my uncle of defrauding me and wanted to investigate how he was conducting his guardianship of my financial affairs. My father was very angry when he heard that I wanted to go back to Austria, but I remained firm and after he had roared and bellowed at me for an hour or more he realized I couldn't be dissuaded.

"So I went back to Austria—and became involved in the Austrian interests I had inherited from my mother. Eventually I married an Austrian girl of good family and —much to my father's disgust and disappointment—settled in Vienna.

"Yet my English education and my acquaintance with English people had left their mark. After my wife died I devoted myself more to my business interests and succeeded in establishing an outlet for my interests in London. After that I often journeyed to and fro between the two countries and occasionally managed to visit Haraldsdyke as well.

"But my father never entirely forgave me for returning to Austria. He had three other sons now by his second marriage, and I was always aware of being a stranger there, a foreigner trespassing on English soil."

He stopped. Flames from the enormous fire nearby roared up the chimney. Hardly liking to interrupt his first long conversation with me I waited for him to continue but when he did not I said puzzled: "And yet he left Haraldsdyke to you when he died."

"Yes," he said, "he left Haraldsdyke to me." He was watching the leaping flames, his face very still. "I knew towards the end that he was disappointed in his three sons by his second marriage, but I never imagined he would cut them out of his will. Yet they received merely nominal bequests when he died."

"Why was that? What had they done to disappoint him?"

He hesitated, fingering his tankard of ale, his eyes still watching the flames. "Ned the youngest was always a sullen, difficult child," he said at last. "No one took much notice of him. He was dark and ungainly and not in the least handsome. Vere, the second son, was too serious and staid, and he and my father could never agree on anything, least of all on how the lands should be farmed. Vere is keenly interested in agriculture and wanted to use new scientific methods which my father thought were a great deal of nonsense. The crowning disaster came when Vere secretly married a village girl, the daughter of the local witch. My father disowned him, then repented and forgave him later. I think in spite of himself my father was impressed by Alice, Vere's wife. She's clever enough not to try to be something she's not, and she's made no effort to adopt a refined speaking voice or wear clothes which are too grand and extravagant. She's quiet, very simple and unaffected in her dress and manner—and at least presentable. Also I believe she's an excellent mother. She's borne Vere five or six children, if my memory is correct. Not all of them have lived, of course, but I think three are surviving so far. However, in spite of the fact that the marriage was not unsuccessful, my father never fully forgave Vere for marrying beneath him."

"And the eldest son," I said. "Why was he a disappointment?"

"Rodric?" A sudden draught made the flames leap up the chimney with a roar again before subsiding beneath the glowing logs. The wind rattled fiercely at the shutters. "Rodric died. It was the day of my father's death. He rode off across the Marsh to Rye and the mists blew in from the sea to engulf him. I went after him but all I found was his horse wandering among the dykes and his hat floating among the rushes near a marshy tract of land. His horse must have missed its footing on the narrow path and thrown him into the boggy waters of the mere."

I shivered, picturing all too vividly the mists of the marshes I had never seen, the twisting path from Haraldsdyke to Rye. "Is there no road, then?" I said in a low voice. "Is there no road which links the house to the town?"

"Certainly, but Rodric didn't want to take the road. He was trying to escape, taking the old path across the road."

It was like that moment in many dreams when a familiar landscape is suddenly contorted without warning into a hideous vista. I had been listening so tranquilly to Axel's narrative that I did not grasp the drift of what he was saying until it met me face to face. The shock made the color drain from my face. I stared at him wordlessly.

"My father died as the result of a blow from the butt of a gun," said Axel quietly, "and it was Rodric who struck the blow."

The landlord came in then to inquire whether our meal was satisfactory and whether there was anything else we required. When he had gone I said: "Why didn't you tell me this before?"

Axel glanced aside. I sensed for a moment that I had come closer than I had ever come to disturbing the smooth veneer of his sophistication. Then he shrugged his shoulders. "The story is past history," he said. "It's over now, the affair closed. It's necessary that you should know of it as you will undoubtedly hear the story from other people, but it need not concern you."

But I felt that it already concerned me. "What brought Rodric to do such a terrible thing?" I said appalled. "I don't understand."

"No," he said. "You would not understand. You never knew Rodric."

"Tell me about him."

"He's dead," said Axel. "You need not concern yourself with his ghost."

"Yes, but—"

"He was as wild and turbulent as Vere was staid and predictable. He was like a child in his ceaseless search for some new adventure which would give him a bizarre sense of excitement. He was always in trouble from an early age, and the older he grew the more he resented his father's power. There was a clash of wills. However, my father tended to favor Rodric and in spite of all his rages did his best to extricate his son from each new scrape in which Rodric found himself. But the relationship deteriorated. In the end my father was threatening to inform the Watch at Rye of Rodric's current activities and swearing he would disinherit Rodric entirely."

"And was it then that Rodric killed him?"

"He was the last to see my father alive and it was

known that they quarreled violently. Part of the conversation was overheard. Directly afterwards he rode off over the Marsh."

"And the gun—"

"It was his own gun. He had been out shooting and had just returned to the house when my father called out to him from the library. Rodric went in to see him, the gun in his hand. I know that to be true, for I had been out shooting with him and was in the hall when my father called out."

"Was it you, then, who found your father dead?"

"No, it was my step-mother who found him. Rodric had already left and Vere had been out all the afternoon on the estate. He didn't come back till later. Then the footman told us that Rodric had gone and I rode after him to try to bring him back. But I was too late."

"And the quarrel—part of it had been overheard, you said?"

"'Yes, by Vere's wife Alice and by my father's ward and god-daughter Mary Moore, whom I don't believe I've mentioned to you before. They were in the saloon adjacent to the library and when my father raised his voice, he could easily be heard through the thickness of an inside wall. After a while they became embarrassed and retired to the drawing-room upstairs. Or at least, Mary did. Alice went off to the nursery to attend to the children."

"And your youngest half-brother Edwin, Ned, where was he? Didn't he hear or see anything?"

"He was in the hay with the second scullery maid," said Axel with a bluntness which startled me. I was reminded with a jolt of the relationship existing between us and the frankness that was now permitted in our conversation with each other. "The entire account of his adolescent escapade was duly revealed at the inquest."

"Inquest!"

"Well, naturally there had to be an inquest. The coroner's jury held that my father had been murdered and that Rodric had met his death by accident while trying to hasten as quickly as possible from the scene of the crime. They also recommended that no blame should be attached to the living for my father's death, so that although as a coroner's jury they were not allowed to judge whether Rodric committed the crime or not, their recommendation was sufficient to tell the world that in their opinion Rodric was guilty."

"I see." I was silent, picturing the inquest, the stuffy courtroom, the stolid jurors, the gaping gossiping crowd. "Was the inquest at Rye?"

"Yes, it was. Fortunately the coroner was a friend of my father's lawyer James Sherman and was anxious to spare us as much as he could, but the affair caused a tremendous amount of gossip and speculation throughout the Cinque Ports. There was even more gossip when the contents of my father's will became known and I discovered, to my acute embarrassment, that he had left everything to me. Everyone was stunned, of course. We all knew that he had threatened to cut Rodric out of his will, but no one had guessed that he had already actually done so. Furthermore, neither Vere nor Ned had had any idea that they too were disinherited. But according to James Sherman, the lawyer, my father had signed the new will on the day before he died."

"But if the inheritance was such an embarrassment to

you," I said, "could you not have renounced it? Or assigned it to your brothers?"

"Yes, I could have done so and in fact I did consider it at first, but then I realized it would be a betrayal of my father's wishes and the trust he had placed in me. He had made this will in a sane rational frame of mind and no doubt had reasons for eliminating his other sons from any share of Haraldsdyke. I felt the least I could do to implement his wishes was to accept the inheritance nominally at least. However, I had my own affairs to manage and it was obvious to me that I could not stay long at Haraldsdyke. The estate was at any rate in the hands of trustees for a year—this was because my inheritance was contingent on my marrying an Englishwoman and was not mine outright until I had fulfilled this condition. I told the trustees, James Sherman and his brother Charles, that I wished Vere to be allowed the practical administration of the estate in my absence, and then I returned to Vienna to arrange my affairs so that I could return to England at the earliest opportunity and seek a suitable wife."

"But supposing you hadn't married," I said. "What would have happened to the estate then?"

"It was willed to Vere's son, Stephen, who is at present a child of three. Even now, if I die without issue, the estate is to pass to Stephen. If Stephen dies childless before the age of twenty-one, his younger brother will inherit—and so on . . . Every contingency is provided for."

"I see." I was silent. "Will you still have to go back to Vienna often?"

"About once a year. I've consolidated and delegated my business interests to enable me to spend most of the year in England."

"And Vere and Alice? What's to happen to them? How they must resent us coming to usurp them!"

"I see no reason why they should be usurped. I would welcome Vere's help in administering the estate for I know nothing of agriculture, and Alice will be able to show you how a country house should be run."

"But how old is Alice?" I said, feeling very insecure indeed. "Won't she be angry when I take her place?"

"You forget," said Axel. "Alice is a simple, plain country girl who has had experience of acting as house-keeper in a large mansion. You are a young woman of an education and background far above her. There won't be any conflict at all. It will be obvious from the beginning that you are the rightful mistress of the house. Alice won't mind in the least—it will give her more time to attend to her children. She's the most excellent mother."

"But the others, your step-mother . . ."

"Esther and I have always been on the best of terms," he interrupted. "She will be glad to see me again and anxious to see that you feel comfortable and at ease at Haraldsdyke. Who else is there? Only Mary, my father's ward, and she is a mere child of fourteen who will be far too busy trying to please her governess to be much concerned with you. You needn't worry about her in the least."

"And Ned," I said. "You've forgotten Ned again."

"Ned? Well, I hardly think he need concern you much either. I think I shall suggest to him that he enlists in the army. He must be nineteen now and it's high time he did something constructive with his life instead of idling it away in the taverns of the Cinque Ports or the haystacks of the Romney Marsh. He's not intelligent enough to go to a University. Any attempt at providing him with further education would be a waste of money." He drained his tankard of ale and took out his watch to glance at it. "I think we should retire soon," he said abruptly. "We have another long day ahead of us tomorrow and you should get plenty of rest to avoid becoming too tired."

"As you wish." I was recalled at once from my thoughts of the past by the dread of the night to come.

"The landlord fortunately has a private room for us both," he said. "So often in these English inns one has to share a communal bedroom even if not a communal bed."

I tried to look pleased.

"Perhaps you will have some wine with me before we retire?" he said. "It's such a damp chill night and the wine will warm us both."

I protested half-heartedly but then agreed readily enough. I would have seized on any excuse to postpone the moment when I would be alone with him in the bedroom.

The wine not only warmed my blood but made me feel drowsy and relaxed. I meant to ask him on the stairs what "activities" Rodric had pursued which would have offended the police at Rye, but my mind was hazy and I was unable to concentrate sufficiently to revive our earlier conversation. Marie-Claire was waiting for me in the bedroom, but I dismissed her at once to her own sleeping quarters for I could see she was greatly fatigued, and undressed as quickly as I could without her. I discovered that she had stretched my nightgown over the warming-pan in the bed, and I felt the luxurious warmth sooth my limbs as the silk touched my skin. A second later I was in bed and lying sleepily back on the pillows.

He had been correct in the assumptions he had made that morning at Claybury Park. Matters did improve; at least this time I was spared the shock of disillusionment. Afterwards he was asleep almost at once, but although I moved closer to him for warmth and even ventured to lay my head against his shoulder he did not stir, and I was conscious even then of his remoteness from me.

The next day we set off early from the inn at Sevenoaks and journeyed further south through the meadows of Kent until we reached the great spa of Tunbridge Wells which Charles II's queen, Henrietta Maria, had made famous over a century and a half before. It is not, of course, as celebrated as Bath, which is famed throughout Europe, but Axel found the town interesting enough to linger in and thought that a short journey that day would be less tiring for me. Accordingly we dined at an excellent tavern near the Pantiles and stayed the night at an inn not far from the Pump Room. Again we shared the same bedroom, but this time it was I who slept first and did not wake till it began to rain at seven the next morning.

We had not spoken again of his family, but as we set out on the last stage of our journey on Wednesday I began to think of them again. I was particularly anxious at the thought of meeting Alice. I hoped she would not be too much older than me so that my disadvantage would not be so great, but if she had had six children already it was probable that she was at least twenty-two or even older.

I began idly to count the months to my eighteenth birthday.

The journey that day seemed never-ending. We progressed along the borders of Kent and Sussex and the rain poured from leaden skies to make a mire of the road. At

several inns we had to stop to allow the coachman to attend to the horses who quickly tired from the strain of
pulling their burden through the mud, and then at last as
we crossed the border into Sussex and left the rich farm-
ing land of Kent behind, the rain ceased and on peering
from the carriage window I saw we were approaching a
new land, a vast tract of green flatness broken only by the
blue ribbon of the sea on the horizon.

"This is the Romney Marsh," said Axel.

It was not as I had imagined it to be. I think I had pictured a series of marshes and bogs which would remind
me of descriptions I had heard of the Fen Country in East
Anglia, but although there were probably marshes and
bogs in plenty, they were not visible from the road. The
grass of the endless meadows seemed very green, and occasionally I glimpsed the strips of farmland, and the hud-
dle of stone buildings. There were no hedges or other en-
closures, but often I could glimpse the gleam of water
where a farmer had cut a dyke to drain his property.

"They plan to drain more of the Marsh," said Axel,
after he had pointed out the dykes to me. "The soil is rich
here if only it can be used. Vere has been experimenting
with crops and growing turnips and other root vegetables
instead of letting a third of the land lie fallow each year.
There have been similar interesting experiments in crop
rotation in East Anglia; I believe the late Lord Town-
shend was very successful in evolving the method, but my
father held out against it for a long time and clung to the
old ways. He distrusted all innovations on principle."

"And was all the Marsh a swamp once?"

"A great deal of it was below the sea at one time, but
that was centuries ago. Up to the fourteenth century Rye

and Winchelsea were the mightiest ports in all England, rivals even to London, and then the sea receded from their walls and the river silted up in Rye harbor so that now they're mere market towns with memories of medieval grandeur."

"And is Hastings nearby—where the Conqueror landed?"

"It's less than ten miles from Winchelsea. The ancestor of the Brandsons was reputedly a Dane called Brand who was in King Harold's entourage and fought with Harold against the Norman invaders."

"My mother's family was descended from Charlemagne," I said, thinking he was becoming too boastful and determined not to be outshone, but to my annoyance he merely laughed as if I had made a joke.

"My dear child," he said amused, "each one of us had an ancestor who was alive a thousand years ago. The only difference between us and, say, our coachman riding behind his horses is that we know the names of our ancestors and he doesn't."

This seemed to me to be a most peculiar observation and I found his amusement irritating in the extreme. I decided the most dignified course of action was to ignore his remark altogether, and accordingly I turned my attentions to the landscape outside once more.

The weather was improving steadily all the time, but now darkness was falling, and as I drew my redingote more tightly around myself I peered through the window to watch the shadows lengthening over the Marsh. The dykes now gleamed mysteriously, the flat ground gave curious illusions of distance and nearness. When I first saw the lights of Rye they seemed very close at hand, a cluster of illuminations dotting the dark rise of a hill, but it was another hour before we were finally below the walls of the town and the horses were toiling up the cobbled road to the great gate at the top of the rise.

"Vere said he would meet us at the Mermaid Inn," said Axel. "The carriage will stop there presently. Ah, here's the high street! You see the old grammar school? My father sent Ned there to learn his letters. Vere had a private tutor but it was hardly worth spending the money on such a luxury for Ned. . . . You can see how old the town is—I would think it probable that the streets and alleys you see now are little changed from the medieval days when they were built."

I stared fascinated out of the window. I had never seen any town like it before, for Cheltenham, where I had spent my schooldays, was now filled with the modern buildings of the eighteenth century, and the parts of London where I had lived were also relatively new. I was reminded of the city of London which lay east of Temple Bar, a section I had seldom visited, but even though there was a similarity between the city and this town, Rye still seemed unique to me as I saw it then for the first time.

The carriage reached the Mermaid Inn in Mermaid Street, the driver halted the horses in the courtyard, and presently I heard the shouts of the ostlers and the sounds of the baggage being unloaded.

My limbs were stiff. As Axel helped me down into the courtyard I slipped and fell against him, but before I could apologize for my clumsiness he said abruptly: "There's Ned, but I see no sign of Vere."

I turned.

There was a man in the doorway of the inn, and as he

saw us he stepped forward so that the light lay behind him and I could not see his face. His movements seemed curiously reluctant.

"Where's Vere?" said Axel sharply to him as he drew nearer to us. "He told me he'd be here to meet us."

"There was an accident." He had a deep voice with more than a hint of a Sussex rural accent. The accent shocked me for I had thought that all gentry, no matter where they lived in England, spoke the King's English. He was not as tall as Axel, but was so powerfully built that he in fact seemed the larger of the two. He had narrow black eyes, a stubborn mouth and a shock of untidy black hair which was cut very short in the manner of a yokel. "The prize bull threw one of the farm hands and Vere rode himself to Winchelsea to get Doctor Salter. He asked me to meet you instead and give you his apologies for not being here as he promised."

"Couldn't he have sent you to fetch the doctor and come here himself to meet us as we arranged?"

"He was too worried about the hand. They fear his back is broken."

"I see." But he was clearly angry. I waited uneasily for him to introduce me, for the man was looking at me openly now with curious eyes.

"Where is the carriage?"

"Over there."

"Then let's waste no more time standing here, or my wife will catch cold." He half-turned to me. "May I introduce my youngest half-brother, Edwin . . . Ned, attend to our baggage, would you? Is Simpson with the carriage? Get him to assist you."

But Ned had taken my hand in his and was bowing low with unexpected ceremony. "Your servant, ma'am."

"How do you do," I said, responding to convention, and then Axel's hand was on my arm and Axel's voice said coolly: "This way, my dear."

If Ned's Sussex accent had worried me about the gentility of the Brandsons, their carriage quickly restored my faith in their social position. It was polished and elaborate, well-sprung and comfortable, and clearly could only have been maintained by a gentleman.

"You were barely civil to Ned," I said in a low voice once I was seated. "Why was that?"

He had been stooping to examine the fastening of the carriage door, but once I spoke he swung around, seeming to tower above me in that small confined space. "He needs discipline," he said abruptly. "My father let him run wild and his mother cannot control him. He shows tendencies of becoming as wild as Rodric but with none of Rodric's charm and grace of manner." He sat down opposite me and the shaft of light from the porch shone directly across his face so that I saw for the first time the anger in his eyes. "And let me tell you this," he said. "I dislike the idea of reproving you so soon after our marriage, but I think I should clearly indicate from the start whenever I find your conduct unsatisfactory. If I was 'barely civil' to Ned, as you put it, that's my affair and has nothing to do with you. I did not ask for your comment, nor did I expect one. Just because you're my wife doesn't give you the liberty to criticize my manners whenever they may appear to your inexperienced eyes to be defective. Do you understand me?"

Tears stung my eyes. "Yes," I said.

"Then we shall say no more about it." He glanced at his watch and put it away again. "We should be at Haraldsdyke within half an hour."

I was silent.

I had expected Ned to join us in the carriage, but he evidently preferred to travel outside with the coachman and the servants, so Axel and I remained alone together. Within twenty minutes of our leaving the inn courtyard, Rye and Winchelsea were mere twin hills pinpricked with lights behind us, and the country on either side of the road was hidden by the darkness of the night. I felt very tired suddenly, and as always when my spirit was at a low ebb I thought of Alexander and longed for his companionship. Axel's anger seemed to have driven a wedge between us and made me feel isolated and alone again.

The darkness hid Haraldsdyke from my eyes. I had half-anticipated passing lodge gates and traveling up a long drive to the house, but there was no lodge, only tall iron gates set in a high weather-beaten wall, and then a sharp ascent to a level above the Marsh. I was to learn later that all the oldest houses on the Marsh were built on a slight elevation of the land above sea-level in order to escape the dangers of floods and spring tides. The carriage drew up before the house, Axel helped me to dismount, and then even before I could strain my eyes through the gloom to make out the shape of the gray walls, the front door was opened and a woman stood on the threshold with a lamp in her hand.

I knew instinctively that it was Alice. My nerves sharpened.

Ned and the coachman were attending to the baggage as Axel led me forward up the steps to the front door, but I had already forgotten them. My whole being was focused on the meeting which lay immediately ahead of me.

"Good evening, Alice," said Axel as we reached her.

"May I present my wife?" And he turned to me and made the necessary counter-introduction.

Alice smiled. She was still plain even then, I noticed with relief. She had brown hair, soft and wispy, and a broad face with high cheekbones and green eyes. She had a heavy peasant's build with wide shoulders and an over-large bosom, and I would have thought her exceedingly fat if I had not realized suddenly that she was perhaps four months pregnant. The image of the meticulously efficient housekeeper and superbly conscientious mother receded a little and I was aware of an enormous relief. She was, after all, merely an ordinary country woman and there was no reason why I should feel inferior to her in any way.

"Why, how pretty you be!" she exclaimed softly, and her accent was many shades thicker than Ned's. "Pray come in and feel welcome . . . Vere's coming, George," she added to Axel, and it gave me a shock to hear him called by the name his father had given him, even though he had warned me about it earlier. "He just returned from Winchelsea and went to change his clothes to receive you."

She led us across a long hall and up a curving staircase to the floor above. Within a moment we were in a large suite of rooms where fires burned in the grates and lamps cast a warm glow over oak furniture.

"I thought you should be having your father's rooms," she said to Axel. "They've not been used since his death, God rest his soul. Your step-mother still has her rooms in the west wing." She turned to me. "Let me know if there's anything more you need," she said. "George mentioned in his letter that you had a maid, and I've arranged for her to sleep in the room across the corridor for the time being. If you'd rather she slept in the servants' wing—"

"No," I said. "That will suit me very well."

"Then if there's nothing more I can do for you at present I'll leave you to refresh yourselves after your journey. The footmen will be up with the luggage in a minute, I dare say, and I've just had the maids bring up some hot water for you—see, over there in the ewers. . . . Would you like me to send any victuals up to you on a tray? Or some nice hot tea?"

I opened my mouth to accept, and then remembered Axel's presence and was silent.

He glanced at me, raising his eyebrows, and when I nodded my head, he said: "Some tea would be excellent, Alice. But please tell the rest of the family that we shall come down to the saloon as soon as possible."

The tea certainly revived me. Presently Marie-Claire arrived and helped me wash and change, and some time later when I was attired in a fresh gown and with my hair re-arranged, I began to take more notice of my surroundings. They were indeed beautiful rooms. It was true that they had not the light elegance of the London drawing-rooms, but each piece of oak furniture was a work of art of previous centuries, and the long velvet curtains at the windows and around the bed added impressiveness to the setting. I pulled aside one of the curtains to glance outside into the night, but it was too dark for me to see anything although I fancied I saw the lights of Rye and Winchelsea twinkling in the distance.

Axel came out of the dressing-room to meet me a few minutes later. His valet had shaved him for the second time that day, and he wore a gray coat with square tails, a striped waistcoat and long beige breeches cut in the

French style which were slit at the sides above the ankle. He looked exceedingly elegant, yet curiously out of place in that quiet English country house. Perhaps, I thought alarmed, I also looked too elegant, even over-dressed, for the occasion. I glanced in the mirror hastily but before I could pass judgment on myself, he said: "Thank God you don't look like Alice!" and kissed the nape of my neck as he stood behind me.

He was evidently trying to make amends for his harshness at Rye. "Am I suitably dressed?" I said, still seeking reassurance. "I would not want to create a wrong impression."

"If you change your dress now I shall be very angry," he retorted. "You need not worry about creating wrong impressions when you look as well as you do now."

We went downstairs to the saloon.

Alice was knitting when we entered the room. I remember being surprised, because all the ladies I had been acquainted with in the past had spent their leisure hours sewing and I had never actually seen anyone knit before. There was a girl next to her on the couch, a lumpy girl with a pimpled face and an air of being near-sighted. This must evidently be Mary, Robert Brandson's ward, whom Axel had mentioned to me. My glance passed from the two plain women to the woman in the high-backed chair by the fireplace, and stayed there. For here was one of the most striking women I had ever seen, not perhaps as beautiful or as attractive as my mother, but a handsome, good-looking woman of about forty-five years of age with black hair tinged with silver at the temples and the wide-set slanting eyes I had noticed earlier when I had first met Ned.

She rose to her feet as we entered the room and

crossed the floor towards us, every movement stressing her domination of the scene.

"Well, George," she said to Axel, "it took you ten months to find an English bride, but I must say the long delay obviously produced the best results! She looks quite charming." She drew me to her and kissed me on both cheeks with cool dry lips. "Welcome to your new home, child."

I disliked being called "child," but nonetheless contrived to curtsey and smile graciously while murmuring a word of thanks to her.

"How are you, Esther," Axel was saying to his step-mother, but he made no attempt to kiss her, and I realized then that he had shown no hint of affection to any member of his family. "You look much better than when I last saw you."

"Please, George, don't remind me of those dreadful days of the inquest . . . Mary, come over here—you're not chained to the couch, are you? That's better . . . my dear, this is Mary Moore, my husband's ward who lives here with us—ah, here's Vere at last! Where have you been, Vere? George and his wife have just come downstairs only a moment ago."

He was a slim pale man. He seemed to have inherited his mother's build, but otherwise he did not resemble her. He had fair hair and lashes, and his complexion was so light that it was almost feminine. In contrast his eyes were a deep vivid blue and were by far his most striking feature; I particularly noticed them because when he smiled it was with his mouth only and his eyes remained bright but without expression.

"Hello George," he said, and while I noticed that he spoke the King's English without trace of a country accent I also noticed that he spoke as he smiled, without expression. "We were beginning to think you weren't returning to Haraldsdyke."

He might have sounded disappointed, but he did not. However, neither did he sound pleased. The curious lack of inflection made me feel uneasy.

I was presented to him, but although he was courteous in his response I still did not feel at ease with him. We all conversed for perhaps ten minutes in that gracious, well-lit room, and then the butler announced that supper was served, and we crossed the hall to the dining room. I was hungry after the long journey, and was glad that they had a light meal waiting for us instead of the customary six o'clock tea. We had dined late that afternoon at an inn somewhere along the Sussex border, and dinner now seemed a long time ago.

There was a chandelier in the dining room and the silver glinted beneath its bright light. Axel went straight to the head of the table without hesitation, but I paused not knowing where I should place myself, anxious not to give offense.

I saw Axel frown and make a barely perceptible gesture to the other end of the table. Moving quickly I went to the chair which he had indicated, and sat down in haste.

There seemed to be a general hesitation which I did not understand. I began to wonder in panic what mistake I could have made, and then Vere, who was immediately on my right, murmured to me: "You do not intend to say grace?"

I was speechless.

"I think it unnecessary to say grace more than once a day," said Axel from the head of the table. "My wife is accustomed to saying grace only at dinner and not on any other occasion."

"Quite right too," said Esther from her place on Axel's right. "Times change. Nowadays I hear only the nonconformists say grace at every meal . . . Mary dear, do try and sit up straighter! What will happen to your figure if you tend to droop so?"

Not much that has not already happened, I thought dryly, and then felt sorry for the poor girl as she flushed in embarrassment and sat up as straight as a ramrod. It occurred to me that Esther had a sharp tongue behind her honeyed voice.

Supper began. We were halfway through the roast beef when the door opened and Ned came into the room. It was the first time I had seen him in a clear light and I was struck by the fact that his clothes were dirty and shabby, and that he obviously had not troubled to change or wash for the meal.

"I'm sorry to be so late," he said. "I was attending to the horses."

There was a slight pause. At the head of the table, Axel laid down his knife and leaned back in his chair.

"Whose job is it to look after the horses?"

Ned stopped, one hand on the back of his chair.

"Well?"

"The grooms."

"Have I employed you to be a groom?"

"No."

"Then in the future you will be punctual at meals and not tend the horses when you should be at the table."

Ned said nothing. I noticed that the tips of his ears were a dull red.

"And I'm afraid I can't allow you to sit down to a meal

looking as unkempt and untidy as a farmhand. You'd better go and eat in the kitchens, and take care to mend your ways in the future, for next time you appear like this in the dining room you'll be thrashed."

The room was very still.

"Do you understand that?"

There was a heavy silence.

"Answer me!"

"Yes," said Ned, "you damned bloody foreigner." And he was gone, the door banging behind him, his footsteps echoing as he crossed the hall towards the kitchens.

The silence was painful. The footmen tried to pretend they were mere statues incapable of sight or hearing; Esther looked horrified; the girl Mary's eyes were almost as round as the dinner-plates on the table before us. On my right, Vere was motionless, his knife still poised in his hand, and beyond him Alice seemed to be inspecting what appeared to be an imaginary spot on the tablecloth.

Axel shrugged his shoulders. "This food is excellent," he observed to no one in particular. "It would be a pity to let it grow cold any longer." And he leaned forward in his chair to resume his meal.

"George," said Esther in distress, "I really feel I must apologize for him—"

"No," said Axel strongly. "That's not necessary. I would not accept any apology which did not come from his own lips. There's no reason why you should assume responsibility for his insults."

"He gets more uncouth daily," was all she said. "I'm beyond knowing what should be done with him."

"He's trying so hard to be a second Rodric," said Vere, "that he has overreached himself and his attempts at emulation have merely resulted in a distorted parody."

"But he is nothing like Rodric!" Esther cried angrily. "Nothing at all!"

"No," said Mary, speaking for the first time. "He is so different from Rodric."

"Rodric had such charm, such wit, such . . ." Esther broke off, and to my discomfort turned to me. "It was the most dreadful tragedy," she said rapidly. "No doubt George has mentioned—"

"Yes," I said. "Axel told me."

"Now, ma'am," said Vere to his mother, "you mustn't upset yourself."

"No, I'm not upset, but it's just that now we're all gathered together again around this table I seem to see Rodric's ghost the whole time—"

"Ah come, Esther," Axel said unexpectedly. "Talking of Rodric's ghost will make you feel no better. We all miss Rodric to some degree, just as we all miss Papa, and certainly you are entitled to miss both of them more than any of us, but dwelling on your loss will only aggravate your grief. You must know that."

"I should like to know," said Vere, "—just out of interest, naturally—which of us had missed Papa."

His voice was extremely polite. While everyone looked at him he cut a slice of beef from the plate in front of him, speared it with his fork and ate it tranquilly.

"Well, of course," said Axel, equally courteous, "we all know there was little love lost between you and Papa, and still less between you and Rodric."

"One might say the same of you," said Vere. "We all know what you apparently thought of Rodric. It was clear from your silence at the inquest that in your opinion Rodric was a murderer."

"Are you suggesting that he wasn't?"

"Why no," said Vere, his blue eyes open wide. "If Rodric didn't kill Papa, then who did?"

There was a clash of a glass shivering into fragments. Alice rose abruptly in dismay, her dress stained with wine from the glass she had overturned. "Dear Lord, look what I've done—"

The diversion was immediate. One of the footmen darted forward with an ineffectual white napkin; the butler murmured "T-t-t-" in distress, and Esther said: "Oh Alice, your new gown!"

"So careless I was," said Alice. "So clumsy. Pray excuse me . . ."

The men rose as she left the table to try and repair the damage, and then seated themselves again.

"Such a pity," said Esther absently. "The stain will never come out." She turned to me without warning. "Well, my dear, tell us more about yourself. George said so little in his letter."

I began to talk, my voice answering her questions naturally, but my mind was confused by the glimpse of the emotions which I had seen unleashed during the earlier conversation, and I found concentration difficult. I was thankful when at last the meal was over and Mary and I retired to the drawing room while Vere and Axel remained in the dining room with their port. Esther had excused herself from us to see if Alice had been able to reduce the stain on her gown, and so Mary and I were alone together.

There was suddenly so little to say. Even though we were only three years apart in age the gulf between us seemed enormous. After five minutes of desperately difficult conversation I seized on the first topic which entered my head.

"If it will not affect you too much," I began cautiously, "please tell me a little about Rodric." That seemed somewhat bold, so I added, lying: "Axel told me he had a remarkable personality."

I could hardly have imagined the effect my words would have. All trace of nervousness seemed to leave the girl; her face was suddenly alive with animation. "George was right," she said. "Rodric was a most remarkable person."

I was prepared to relax now that I had discovered a topic on which we might both converse for a time, but I did not. Something in her manner was so unexpected that I felt my nerves sharpen more than ever in my effort to discern the truth.

"Mr. Brandson—my guardian—was most anxious that I—that Rodric and I . . ." She blushed, hesitated a little. "Of course, I was then too young for any formal mention of it to be made, but it was intended that Rodric and I . . ." She paused delicately.

I stared at her. "You mean Mr. Brandson wished you both to be betrothed when you were old enough?"

"Well, yes . . . yes, he wished, hoped . . ." Her hands worked nervously at her dress. "I am orphaned now, as you no doubt know, but my father was a baronet with an estate in Hampshire and I have a considerable portion which he willed to me . . . It would have been a suitable match." Her pale eyes misted slightly. She turned her head aside with a sharp movement as if to hide her emotions.

"I see," I said, trying not to sound too amazed.

"Rodric was so noble," she said. "He was such a fine upright worthy person. Fond as I was of my guardian, I sometimes think that on many occasions he did not treat Rodric as he deserved."

"I heard," I said, "that they often didn't see eye to eye."

"My guardian was so blind, so prejudiced . . . Rodric is —was—unusually gifted."

"Gifted?"

"He wrote," said Mary. "He was never happier than when he had a pen between his fingers and an inkwell and paper on the table before him. He wrote mostly articles and political tracts—he concerned himself very much with politics and used to ride as far afield as Dover to speak for the Cause." Seeing that I looked blank she added: "The Whig Cause. It was a dreadful disappointment to my guardian who hoped Rodric would support the Tories and become a member of that party in Parliament. But my guardian didn't understand Rodric, didn't understand that Rodric couldn't acquiesce in accepting ideals he didn't believe in."

But I was more interested in Rodric's possible literary talent than in his possible noble soul. "Did he write any novels?"

"Only one—I read part of it and thought it excellent."

"What was it about? Where's the manuscript? May I read it?"

Her expression changed. "No," she said flatly. "Vere burned all the manuscripts after Rodric's . . . death."

In the pause that followed the door opened and Esther entered the room. Remembering her distress when the subject of Rodric had been introduced at dinner I knew that it would be impossible to continue the conversation with Mary. Apparently Mary had drawn the same conclusions, for she was already moving across the room in search of her sewing basket. "Alice managed to remove most of the stain from the dress," Esther said as she sat down by the fire. "She knows so many of these old wives' recipes! I believe she has a secret recipe for everything, from curing hay fever to making toadstool poison to feed the mice in the cellar. These village girls have an amazing knowledge of such things."

I was aware again of the honeyed tones which did not quite conceal the barbed sharpness of her tongue.

"She has just gone to the nursery to look in on the children," Esther was observing, and suddenly the slanting black eyes were turned in my direction. "Alice," she said, "is the most excellent mother."

I smiled politely, not fully understanding the sudden intentness of her gaze.

"Mary dear," said Esther, "just run down to the saloon and fetch my shawl, would you? I'm a little chilled."

The girl departed obediently.

"I did not quite gather, my dear," said Esther after a moment, "how long you and George have been married."

"Only a week."

"Ah." She picked up a copy of the "Spectator" idly and began to glance through the pages. "And have you known him long?"

"About a month."

"I see." She went on looking at the magazine. "So you don't know him well."

"Well enough," I said, "by this time."

She must have read some meaning into my words which I did not intend, for she glanced up sharply, her beautiful mouth curving in a smile, her unusual eyes sparkling with amusement. "Yes," she said, "I've no doubt you do. If George had anything in common with Rodric, it was his talent for making himself extremely well known to any woman he fancied in the shortest possible time."

If I had been less angry I might have thought how odd it was that Rodric's name was spoken so often in this house, but I was too incensed by the implications of her remark to notice this at the time. I sat facing her, she a poised woman well accustomed to the intricacies of drawing room conversation, I perhaps thirty years her junior but much too furious to be intimidated by her maturity and experience.

"All young men need to sow their wild oats," I said coolly, repeating a phrase my father had often used. "If Axel hadn't sown his in his youth I would have thought him strange indeed. I hardly think I need add that his behavior towards me has always been exemplary in every respect."

"Of course," said Esther. "Naturally." She smiled. "No doubt he now wishes to settle down and be a satisfactory husband. And father."

I did not answer.

"He is anxious for children, of course?"

I was certainly not going to tell her it was a subject we had never discussed.

"Yes," I said, "especially now that he owns Haraldsdyke."

The door opened. I glanced up, expecting to see Mary returning with the shawl, but it was Alice who stood on the threshold. She had changed her gown, and the style did not flatter her condition so that her pregnancy was very obvious.

I had a sudden, inexplicable longing to escape from that room and those women.

"Will you excuse me?" I said politely to Esther. "I am afraid the long journey has made me more than usually tired. I think it best if I retired to bed now."

They were both extremely solicitous. Of course I should rest and recover my strength. Was there anything either of them could do for me? Anything which could be sent up to my room from the kitchens? Could I find my way back to my room unaided?

"We so want you to feel at home here," said Alice. "We so want you to feel welcome."

I thanked her, assured them there was nothing further I needed, and escaped as courteously as possible with a candle in my hand to light the way down the long corridors.

I reached the door of our suite of rooms without difficulty and then paused as I heard the sound of voices raised in argument. The door of the sitting room, or boudoir, was ajar and a shaft of light slanted out across the dark passage before me.

I stopped.

"You think too much of Rodric," I heard Axel say, and his voice was harsh and cold. "It's time you stopped idolizing his memory and saw him as he really was. You're nineteen and yet you behave like a young schoolboy moonstruck by the current School Hero. Rodric wasn't the saint you imagine him to be, neither was he the crusader in shining armor, fighting for truth. He was a misfit who could not or would not conform."

"You were always jealous of him." Ned's voice was low and trembling. "You pretended to be friendly so that he was deceived, but you never liked him. You were Fa-

ther's favorite until you went back to Vienna and then
when you returned later on you found Rodric had taken
your place. You resented him from the moment you saw
he meant more to Father than you did—"

"What childish nonsense you talk!"

"And you hated Father for rejecting you because you
chose to live in Vienna—you wanted to pay him back at
all costs—and pay Rodric back for usurping you . . ."

"I'm beginning to think you want another thrashing. Be
very careful, Ned. You forget I still have the whip in my
hand."

"You can't frighten me! You can beat me and sneer at
me and send me away into the army, but I'll still spit in
your face, you bloody murderer . . ."

There was the stinging vibration of leather on flesh, a
sharp cry of pain.

"You knew Father had altered his will in your favor so
you killed him with Rodric's gun and then pushed Rodric
in the Marsh before he could deny the charge!"

The whip struck again. I listened transfixed, unable to
move. Then:

"You liar," said Axel between his teeth. "You . . ."
And he used words I had once overheard my father use,
syllables never used in civilized conversation.

Ned was half-sobbing, half-laughing. It froze me to
hear him. "Deny it as much as you wish!" he shouted.
"Curse as much as you please! But who inherited
Haraldsdyke when Father died? Who inherited all the
land and the money? Who had the best reason for wanting Father dead?"

"Get out! Get out, do you hear? Get out of my—"

"Not Rodric, George Brandson! And Rodric never
killed him! Rodric wasn't a murderer!"

There was the sound of a scuffle, the impact of fist against flesh, a small spent sigh and then a jarring thud as if something very heavy had slumped to the floor.

Silence fell.

Very softly, almost unaware of my own actions I crept forward, snuffed my candle and hid behind the curtains that concealed the window at the far end of the corridor.

The silence seemed to go on and on without ending.

At last after an interval which seemed to endure as long as an eternity, the door opened and through a chink in the curtains I saw Axel walk away down the passage to the head of the stairs. His head was bent, his shoulders stooped and he moved slowly.

I went at once to the room. Ned was sprawled half-conscious on the carpet, the blood soiling his black hair as it oozed from a cut above his temple. As I knelt beside him and reached for his pulse he groaned and stirred feebly, so I poured him a glass of water from the pitcher in the bedroom and tried to help him to drink.

He opened his eyes and looked so ill that I thought he was going to vomit. Hastening into the bedroom again I seized the chamber pot, which was the first receptacle that I could think of, and brought it to him just in time.

Afterwards he started to tremble. He was chalk-white with the nervous reaction from the scene and as I helped him drink from the glass he seemed very young and defenseless, very frightened and alone. He seemed utterly different now to the enraged defiant accuser whom I had overheard earlier and I suspected he had only spoken in that manner out of bravado.

I was reminded of Alexander; my heart ached suddenly.

"I slipped," he said. "I was trying to hit George when I

slipped, fell and hit my head." His voice was little more than a whisper and his eyes were dark with humiliation. Then: "What are you doing here? Leave me alone." He wrenched himself free, and as I stared at him with mute sympathy he stumbled towards the couch where his coat lay and dressed himself with shaking fingers.

"Why did you let Axel beat you?" I said at last. "You could have struggled and escaped."

"I did struggle," he said wryly, "and fell and cut my head." He sat down abruptly. I guessed that he was feeling dizzy again after his experience, and I went to him, as I would have gone to Alexander, and put my arm around his shoulders to comfort him.

He recoiled instantly. "Don't," he muttered.

"I only want to help you."

"I shall be well in a minute. Leave me alone." He looked at me suddenly. "George would be angry," he whispered. "He would be angry with you. Don't let him see you with me."

His eyes were bright with tears. I saw then that he was desperately afraid of Axel and terrified at the memory of the scene which had just passed. And as I stared at him in appalled silence there were voices far off in the distance and footsteps resounding in the corridor.

"Please go," he said. "Please."

"Certainly not," I said. "These are my rooms and I have a right to be here. I'm not afraid." But I moved away from him all the same, and my legs were strangely unsteady as I rose to my feet.

The door opened.

Vere came into the room followed by Axel. They both stopped short when they saw me.

I stood my ground, my head erect, my mouth dry, and looked Axel straight in the eyes.

"I came here a moment ago from the drawing room," I said. "Do you wish that I should return there until you have finished whatever business you have to discuss with Ned?"

After a moment, Axel said: "No, that won't be necessary. Vere has merely come to help Ned to his room."

Ned started to tremble again. For a moment I feared he might faint, but he seemed to recover a little. As I watched, Vere crossed the room to him.

"Have you nothing to say to George?"

There was a terrible silence. Ned's eyes were black coals in his white face.

"I've told Vere you are to leave at dawn," Axel said without expression. "I shall give you fifty guineas and then you can make your own way in the world. After all you've said to me I hardly think you would want to live beneath my roof a day longer."

There were tears streaking Ned's face suddenly, great silent tears, and then the harsh sobs tore at his throat and he sank down on the couch, his head in his hands, and wept as if his heart would break.

I could not bear it. He was Alexander to me then, even if he did not resemble Alexander physically. I ran across the room and pressed him close to me and begged him not to cry.

Axel called my name.

I stood up and went to him without hesitation. "Don't send him away," I said. "Please don't send him away. He didn't mean what he said to you, I'm sure. He was much too upset and unhappy to say meaningful things."

"Go into the other room," was all he said. "This is not a matter in which you need involve yourself."

"Please," I said, and I could feel the tears in my own eyes now. "My brother would often say stupid foolish things when he was in a rage, and afterwards he would regret them bitterly. My brother—"

"Your brother is at Harrow, ma'am, and Ned is a stranger whom you do not know. Now be so kind as to retire and leave us together."

But before I could move Ned spoke from the other side of the room. "It's as she says." His voice shook a little, but he was on his feet again without swaying, the tears wet on his cheeks. "I didn't mean what I said, George. It was all lies—all wickedness . . . suddenly I missed Rodric so much that I allowed my grief to cloud my mind and said terrible things which I knew were untrue. . . . Please forgive me and don't send me away. Tell me how I can apologize to you and make amends for what I said, for I swear before God in all truth that I'm sorry for everything I've done to offend you this evening and want only to act better in future."

There was a silence.

"Please, Axel, please don't send him away—"

"My dear," said Axel to me in a voice of ice. "I have asked you twice to leave the room. I trust I do not have to ask you a third time."

I curtsied wordlessly and went through into the bedroom where I immediately pressed my ear to the panel of the closed door. But the panels were thick, and although I could hear the murmur of voices I could not distinguish what was being said. Presently I sat down at my dressing table and began fidgeting idly with the silver brushes and

combs, but my mind was numb and my thoughts became
confused when I tried to think clearly. It occurred to me
then how exhausted I was. Marie-Claire had laid out my
night clothes so I undressed as quickly as possible and
was just sitting before the mirror in my nightgown and
brushing my hair when the murmur of voices ceased, a
door closed far away and the next moment Axel himself
came into the room.

I felt afraid suddenly. I could not look at him. But to
my relief he went through to his dressing room without
speaking, and I was left alone to brush out my hair and
creep between the sheets of the huge double bed.

But still my nerves would not let me sleep. My limbs
began to ache with tension and then at last he came back
into the room and slid into bed beside me.

I had of course expected him to reprove me for my
forward behavior in the sitting room when I had tried to
comfort Ned; I had also half-expected some sort of explanation of the scene there, or at least a comment on
what had happened. But he said nothing.

I waited rigid, scarcely daring to breathe, but he was
silent beside me, so motionless that I felt I dared not
move either. After a while the loneliness was even greater
than my fear and muddled bewilderment. I whispered his
name.

He turned sharply. "I thought you were asleep! What's
the matter?"

"Oh Axel, I didn't mean to make you angry, I didn't
mean it, I promise—" Exhaustion made me tearful; my
voice broke a little and forced me to silence.

"My dear child," he said astonished. "Who spoke of
me being angry with you? My anger was directed against
other people and my mind was occupied with other

things." And he drew me to him in an abrupt, not unkind way and kissed me on the forehead. "This has been a difficult evening for you," he said at last, "but I must insist that you don't worry about matters which concern me alone. The problem of Ned is entirely my responsibility and there is absolutely no need for you to share it."

"Is—is he to be sent away?"

"Not at present. He has apologized for his lies and his abuse and has promised to mend his ways. He is, after all, merely an overgrown schoolboy who has never been accustomed to any discipline at all from his family. Now, go to sleep and stop your worrying, and you'll see how much better everything will seem when you wake tomorrow morning."

But when I slept at last I dreamed turbulent nightmares, and saw Rodric drowning in the Marsh while Vere clapped his hands in glee and Alice whispered "We must make the toadstool poison to feed the mice in the cellar;" and suddenly Axel was standing smiling in the hall of Haraldsdyke and Esther was handing him a gun smeared with blood, and Mary was saying to me: "Rodric was such a wonderful murderer, you see." And the word *murderer* seemed to reverberate until its echo filled the hall, and all at once Ned was chasing me to my death in the marshes and calling after me in Alexander's voice: *Axel killed him! Axel's a murderer, a murderer, a murderer . . .*

But when I woke up gasping with the sweat moist on my forehead I found myself alone with the sun shining peacefully through the curtains and Axel's laugh ringing in my ears as he joked with his valet in the dressing room next door.

Three

FROM THE WINDOW I had my first view south across the Marsh in daylight, the flat expanse of green ending in the blue line of the sea not far away, the twin towns of Rye and Winchelsea seeming very near as they basked in the pale autumn sunshine. It was all so peaceful, so serene. I turned aside, feeling strangely reassured, and rang for Marie-Claire.

However presently I was aware that I was not as strong as I had anticipated and I slipped back to bed.

"Ask for a tray to be sent up to me," I told Marie-Claire in French. "I would like some coffee, very black, and a thin slice of burned toast."

She departed for the kitchens.

I was just lying back on the pillows and thinking that if all was well I would be sufficiently recovered by the afternoon to dress and go downstairs, when Axel returned to the room.

"How are you this morning?" He came over to the bed and stooped to kiss me on the lips. Some element in his expression when he looked at me seemed to suggest he found my appearance pleasing in the extreme, but although before I would have felt gratified I now felt an inexplicable desire to remain beyond his reach.

"I'm feeling a trifle delicate this morning," I replied truthfully. "I wondered if you might apologize to the rest of the family for me and say I shall come downstairs this afternoon."

"You're the mistress of the house," was all he said. "You need not excuse your absence to anyone except me. And I, of course, am merely sorry to hear you're indisposed. Perhaps I should send someone to Winchelsea to ask Dr. Salter to come and see you . . ."

"No, no—it's nothing really. I shall be quite recovered in two or three hours. I just feel somewhat tired and would prefer to remain in bed a little longer."

"I understand." He kissed me again and stood up. "I have business to do," he said abruptly. "Vere and I will be riding to Rye this morning to see my father's lawyer James Sherman. There's a possibility that we may be some time."

"I see. Will you be dining at Rye?"

"Possibly. It depends how long our business takes . . . I shall tell Alice you're indisposed and ask her to continue to supervise the household today."

"Oh yes . . . yes, thank you." I had forgotten I was supposed to be in charge of running the house now. After Axel had gone, I lay thinking about the difficulties of assuming a large responsibility about which I knew very little of practical value. I was just wondering if Alice would not perhaps like to continue to supervise the more mundane household details when there was a knock on the door, and Alice herself appeared.

"George told me you weren't well," she said anxiously. "We were all so sorry . . . if there's anything I can be doing for you—" She paused inquiringly.

I repeated the assurance that I had given Axel that I would soon be quite well, but Alice still seemed anxious.

"If you feel at all sick," she said, "I have an excellent herb recipe which I often take during the early months."

I saw she had misunderstood. "No, no," I said, feeling slightly embarrassed. "It's not a question of—" I stopped.

"You're sure? of course you haven't been married long, but sometimes . . . But if you're quite sure that there can be no question of such a thing—"

"Absolutely positive," I said so firmly that she evidently realized at last why I had decided to rest for a few hours further, and at that moment Marie-Claire entered the room with the coffee and burned toast.

I half-hoped Alice would leave then, but she must have thought I needed companionship for she sat down on the chair by the bed and began to talk of the menu she had planned for dinner that evening.

"I hear Vere and Axel may not be here for dinner," I said.

"There will still be ourselves, Vere's mother, Mary and Ned. Unless Ned stays away. He saddled a horse early this morning and rode off over the Marsh."

I was silent.

"Vere says," said Alice, "there was an unfortunate to-do last night between Ned and George."

"I believe everything is all settled now."

"Poor Ned," said Alice. "He does miss Rodric so." She gathered up her skirts and began to rise to her feet. "Well, I must go and see the children and let you rest—"

"No—please," I said suddenly. "Stay and talk for a while—if you can spare the time, of course . . . I am anxious to hear more about Rodric. Everyone seems to have been so fond of him."

Alice hesitated and then sat down again, rearranging her skirts carefully. "Yes," she said, "everyone was so fond of Rodric. Both his parents preferred him to Vere. Vere's mother doted on Rodric and wouldn't even hear a word against him."

"Not even when he got into trouble?" I remembered Axel's references to Rodric's wildness and the Watch at Rye.

Alice's green eyes widened. "You heard about that?"

"Axel mentioned it."

"Ah." She hesitated. Then: "There was nothing Rodric wouldn't dare do," she said. "He was bold. Nothing was sacred, nothing beyond his reach. He used to act the highwayman for his own amusement till rumor reached the ears of the Lord Warden of the Cinque Ports. But nothing was proved against him. At the end he was with the smugglers, working with Delancey the great French smuggler, and in the night he would ride to Dungeness and dodge the Revenue Men on the watch there."

I was amazed. "This was common knowledge?"

"It—was revealed at the inquest . . . Rodric used to despise Vere because Vere would have none of his childish pranks. Highwaymen and smugglers indeed! Such play-acting! Vere was more of a man than he was. I always thought so from the beginning, even when they were boys."

"You knew him then?"

"Yes, I lived in the little village of Haraldsford a mile from here. My mother is a witch." She said it as prosaically as I might have said: "My mother was French." "Rodric and his big rough friends rode up to our cottage one morning and ducked my mother in the witch's ducking-stool over the village pond. They thought it a great joke. My mother put a curse on him afterwards and prayed he would die by water within ten years." She was very sedate, very undisturbed. "He died in the Marsh nine and a half years later," she said. "I wasn't altogether surprised." She straightened the coverlet absentmindedly. "Vere was quite different," she said. "He was always serious and eager to acquit himself well in whatever he undertook. He came to my mother when he was sixteen and asked for a spell which would make all the girls fall in love with him instead of with Rodric." She smiled suddenly, her broad face lightening with humor. "My mother said: 'Here is a girl who cares nothing for Rodric' and led him straight to me. We were very happy, right from the beginning."

"But how old were you then?"

"Thirteen. It was two years before we could be wed, and then Vere's father nearly killed him when he heard the news of our marriage. He wouldn't speak to Vere for two months and Vere worked on a neighbor's farm as a hired hand as his father wouldn't have him at Haraldsdyke. Then I was with child and the winter was cold and Vere sent word to his father asking if he wanted his first grandchild to die of starvation and cold, and so we returned to Haraldsdyke. But the baby died," she said, all trace of humor vanishing from her face. "Poor little thing. He only lived a few hours."

I murmured something sympathetic.

"It was hard for Vere at Haraldsdyke," she said after a while. "Nothing he ever did was right. His father would shout and roar at Rodric, but it was Rodric he loved the best. He never took any trouble to listen to Vere."

"How strange," I said, "that Rodric, whom everyone says was so delightful and charming, never married."

"Yes," she said dispassionately. "He was very handsome. He was tall and strong with a straight back and flat stomach, and his hair was dark as a crow's wing. But his complexion was fair. He had blue eyes, as blue as Vere's, and an easy smile and when he laughed, everyone laughed with him."

I was just deciding that after giving such an attractive description she must have been fonder of him than I had supposed when I saw the hate glitter unmistakably in her eyes.

My heart bumped unevenly with the shock, but she was already looking away. "Yet he never married," she was saying. "He was too busy trying to seduce other men's wives." And as I stared at her she shrugged and smiled again as if to make light of the entire conversation. "He was like that," she said. "It was no fun for him to get a woman who was easy. Everything had to be difficult so that the experience could be turned into a game, a sport, some new prank to amuse him. He was like that."

There was a silence. Then:

"Like the day he died, for instance," she said, and there was a distant expression in her eyes now and I guessed she was seeing other scenes of months ago. "It was Christmas Eve. George had arrived from Vienna three days earlier to spend Christmas with us, and this pleased Vere's father who had had an argument with

Vere over the estate and discovered Rodric was up to some fresh nonsense; I think it was then old Mr. Brandson turned to George.

"I was in the parlor on the morning of Christmas Eve to prepare the menus for Christmas Day and Boxing Day. Rodric found me there. I saw at once that he was anxious for sport—any sport—which would relieve his boredom, but I was expecting Vere to join me and I knew he wouldn't be long. When Vere came minutes later he found me struggling with Rodric and crying for help.

"I have never seen Vere so angry. He would have tried to kill Rodric, I think, but George was with him and restrained him. Then George took Rodric out shooting over the Marsh and they were gone from the house till late afternoon.

"Vere went out afterwards; he had business to attend to on the estate and didn't return to the house till much later. That was a terrible day! I shall never forget when Vere returned to the house and I had to tell him his father was dead."

"I suppose Rodric had already gone by then?"

"Why, yes, Rodric had gone and George had gone too, to try to bring him back. Rodric left the house directly after he quarreled with his father—after his father was dead, we learned later. Esther, Vere's mother, found Mr. Brandson perhaps quarter of an hour after Rodric had gone to the stables and, according to Ned who was there at the time, saddled his horse in haste and rode off into the winter dusk. Poor woman! I heard her screams even though I was in the nursery with the children and I ran at once to the hall."

"It must have been a fearful shock for her."

"Indeed it was. Fortunately George was close at hand,

for he and Mary reached Esther before I did. Mary had been in the drawing room while I had gone to the nursery. To begin with we were in the saloon downstairs by the library but then when Rodric began to quarrel with his father in the library we became embarrassed being as we could hear so clearly through the wall. Mr. Brandson's voice when he was roused was louder than the Town-Crier at Rye, and Rodric's not much quieter."

I longed to ask her what she had overheard but had no wish to appear too inquisitive.

"I suppose Mr. Brandson had challenged Rodric about his relationship with the smugglers," I said carelessly.

"There was rather more said than that," said Alice.

"Oh."

There was a pause. Alice rearranged herself comfortably in her chair. "'Mr. Brandson swore he would disinherit Rodric without delay,' she said. "He swore he would alter his will."

"But hadn't he already done so?"

"Yes, that was strange. I expect George told you that in fact Mr. Brandson had altered his will shortly before his death to disinherit all his sons save George himself. But no one knew that at the time of his death. When Rodric faced his father that afternoon he must still have thought himself due to inherit the money and property one day, and Mr. Brandson never told him he was already disinherited."

"Wasn't it considered strange that Mr. Brandson disinherited his other sons like that?"

Alice shrugged. "He never really favored George," was all she said. "I don't know what made him draw up a will such as the one he made before he died—the will where he left George everything. He and George were never close after George went against his wishes and returned to Vienna."

There was a knock at the door. I was so deeply engrossed in the conversation that I was unaware of the knock until Alice called out: "Who is it?"

"Mary. The rector's wife has called, Alice, and is downstairs in the morning room. Shall I tell her—"

"I shall see her." Alice stood up. "Our church is at Haraldsford," she said to me, "and the parish includes the villages of Haraldsmere and Conyhurst-in-the-Marsh. I expect we shall have several visits this morning from people who wish to call upon you and welcome you to Haraldsdyke. I'll explain that you're indisposed and ask them to call again later."

"If you would—thank you, Alice . . . and please give the rector's wife my apologies."

"Of course." She smiled reassuringly. "Don't you worry yourself about anything. I'll see to anything that needs attending to."

I relaxed in relief as she left the room, and settled down in bed to try and sleep a little more but the more I tried to sleep the more I thought of my conversation with her. Curiously enough, the part which remained most vividly in my mind was her description of Rodric. I could imagine him so clearly now, gay and careless, his zest for life equaled only by his zest for excitement, superbly free of all restrictive ties and the dreariness of responsibilities. The very picture of him stirred my blood. That was the kind of man I would have married if I had had the choice, I thought. Axel's cool sophistication and remoteness of manner was oppressive to me, and the great gulf of the years between us was stifling in the extreme. It occurred to me for the first time that I resented the discipline he already exercised where I was concerned, his bland assumption that I would do as he told me without question. It was true, I thought, that a woman must be submissive in some respects for in many matters the husband was sure to know best, but surely in this day and age she had a certain measure of freedom . . .

For when I was young the nineteenth century had barely begun, and I could not foresee then the great changes of the Victorian era and the dwindling of all women's independence.

Perhaps they had different ideas now in Europe, I thought. Perhaps Axel treated me in this way because he was a foreigner.

The morning passed slowly; I became restless and impatient, and finally at noon I summoned Marie-Claire and began to dress.

Some reason made me long to explore my new home on my own. I did not want Alice, or worse still Axel's step-mother Esther conducting me through each room in a formal tour of inspection. Accordingly when I was dressed I did not go down to the morning room or the saloon, but up the back stairs to the attics beneath the eaves, and when I paused at last it was at the top of the house before a small window which looked out due east across the Marsh. Someone had carved on the windowpane with a diamond. Stooping so that I might see the inscription more clearly I read:

"God Save Englande and Ye Towne of Rye
"God Save Rodric Who Here Did Lye
"Imprisoned."
"JULY 1797"

It was the year of my birth. He would have been about ten or eleven years old, locked in the attic for a while perhaps as punishment for some childhood prank. I wondered where he had found the diamond, and then casting my eye around the little room I saw the huge boxes containing heaven knows how many disused clothes and other articles. Perhaps he had found some long-lost diamond by chance and seized upon it to amuse himself as he whiled away the long hours of imprisonment.

It seemed sad to think that he was dead. I traced the carving on the glass with my fingers, and suddenly he was so real to me that I would hardly have been surprised to turn and find him waiting at the door.

But when I turned there was no one there.

I shook myself impatiently and retraced my steps downstairs again, past the stairs leading to the servants' wing to the floor where Axel and I had our rooms. I stood on the landing, still undecided whether I should go down to the ground floor and risk meeting Alice or Esther, and then at length I turned down the corridor and began glancing inside the rooms which I passed. Several were empty. One I was about to enter and then I heard the murmur of voices so I hastily passed on again. One of the voices I seemed to recognize as the girl Mary's. Perhaps she was doing lessons with her governess.

Life perhaps would not be so unpleasant as a governess, I thought. No strange new relations to meet and satisfy, no mansion suddenly thrust into one's control, no husband whom one was nervous of displeasing. A governess could always leave her employment to seek a better position if she were unhappy. A wife could not leave her husband and home.

I reached the end of the corridor and paused to look back. I had a stifling feeling of being trapped then, a tremor of horror which swept over me in sickening waves.

I would be here for the rest of my life at Haraldsdyke, and the future yawned before me, decade after decade of nothingness. I was only seventeen. I was still so young. Far too young to be trapped in an old house with a group of strangers who might or might not resent me, far too young to be shackled to a man I did not understand and certainly did not love.

It was not that I was afraid of him, I told myself. Merely that I was uneasy in his presence.

I was too frightened then to admit my fear and look it squarely in the face.

Reaching out blindly in an attempt to break my train of thought I opened the door at the end of the corridor and went into the room beyond.

There was a four-poster in one corner and by the window stood a huge oak desk massively carved. The room seemed quiet, unoccupied. I sat down on the chair by the window, my elbows on the desk, and stared out across the Marsh beyond.

It would be better when Alexander came down from Harrow. Perhaps we could even journey to London together for a few days. If Axel allowed it. If I managed to escape pregnancy.

The thought of pregnancy terrified me. I felt as if I were totally unready to face further unknown ordeals, and I had no desire to bear Axel's children.

I wished desperately then that I could talk to someone of my fears, but I knew as soon as the wish became a conscious thought that there was no one in whom I could confide. Even a parson would be horrified by my revulsion against pregnancy; I could almost hear the unknown rector of Haraldsford say shocked: "But marriage is for the procreation of children . . ."

But there were obviously ways of avoiding pregnancy, I thought. Otherwise my mother would have had other children besides Alexander and myself.

Perhaps a doctor . . . I almost laughed in contempt at myself for thinking of the idea. I pictured what the family doctor at Winchelsea would say if I were to ask him if there was a way in which I might avoid producing an heir for Haraldsdyke. He would go straight to Axel.

I was aware of fear then, the sharp prickle beneath my scalp, the sudden moistness of my palms. How absurd, I thought, trying to be angry with myself. I was never afraid of Axel until . . . Until I heard Ned accuse Axel of murder; until I realized later that Axel had the means, motive and opportunity to murder Robert Brandson last Christmas Eve at Haraldsdyke . . .

But Rodric had killed his father, Rodric who had apparently enjoyed life so much, yet had destroyed life in a fit of rage . . .

"I don't believe it," I said aloud to the silent walls of Haraldsdyke. "I don't believe Rodric killed his father. I don't believe it."

My heart was beating very fast. I sat frozen into immobility behind the great desk, my eyes seeing not the isolated sweep of the Marsh beyond the window, but the abyss which was opening before me, the ground which was crumbling beneath my feet. And as I sat there, my whole being locked in a paralysis of panic, the immense silence was broken by the sound of footsteps in the passage and the next moment the door was opening and someone was entering the room.

I whirled around as if the Devil himself had come in search of me, but it was only Robert Brandson's ward, the girl, Mary Moore.

She was wearing a pink muslin gown and the color did not flatter her ungainly figure. Her hair was lank and was fast uncurling itself so that her ringlets were wispy and awry. I could not help wondering if she had been telling me the truth about an unofficial engagement to Rodric.

"Oh!" she exclaimed, much taken-aback, and stared at me in astonishment. "What are you doing here?"

She made it sound as if I were trespassing.

"What are *you* doing here?" I retorted lightly. "It isn't your room, is it?"

There was a pause. Then:

"It was Rodric's room," she said at last. "I come here sometimes."

I stared. And then suddenly I was looking at the room around me, the silent four-poster, the mute walls, the shelf of books which I had not even troubled to examine. I stood up, conscious of feeling uneasy sitting in the chair which he must often have used, my hands on the desk at which he must so often have written.

"I didn't know," I said, "that I was in Rodric's room."

She too seemed awkward and ill-at-ease. She had come to the room to sit for a while and remember him, and instead of meeting her memories she had discovered a stranger trespassing in a place she loved. I felt sorry for her.

"I must go," I said abruptly. "I was only exploring the house. I don't know why I stopped here."

She moved to let me pass, her cheeks flushed with her own embarrassment, her eyes averted from mine, and without reason I stopped, my hand on the door-knob.

"May I ask you something very personal?" I heard myself say suddenly.

She looked up startled. "What's that?"

"You were fond of Rodric. Do you honestly believe he killed his father?"

Her eyes widened. She was evidently stunned and appalled at my frankness and for a long moment she was incapable of speech.

"Come," I said, "tell me, for I'm curious to know. I find it hard to believe from what I've heard of him that Rodric could commit such a cold-blooded murder. Do you think he killed your guardian?"

She licked her pale lips, her eyes still wide and frightened. Then: "No," she whispered. "No, I never believed it. Never."

She was infatuated with him, I told myself. She idolized him. This was not an unexpected answer.

"Then who killed your guardian?" I said.

She looked at me as if I were some hideous monster. "I dare not say."

"Ah, come, Mary! Tell me!"

She shook her head.

"I won't tell anyone, I promise."

"No," she said, "no, I can't tell you. I have no proof, no way of knowing for certain. All I know is that Rodric never killed him. I never believed he did."

"Have you proof that Rodric didn't kill him?"

She shook her head.

"Well, then—" I said exasperated, and then controlled myself. I turned aside. She knew nothing and was of no use to me. "I must go," I said. "Pray excuse me."

I opened the door.

"Alice and I were in the saloon," she said suddenly, the words tumbling from her lips. "Rodric and Godfather were quarreling so loudly that Alice said we should withdraw upstairs."

"Yes, she told me." I opened the door a little wider.

"But she listened eagerly enough," said the girl, and the spite in her voice made me halt and look back at her. "Until Vere's name was mentioned. Then she suggested we should withdraw."

"What did Mr. Brandson say about Vere?"

"I suppose he was comparing Vere to Rodric. He said that although Vere had married beneath him and was a disappointment in many ways, Vere at least wasn't a constant source of embarrassment. Alice stood up as soon as she heard the phrase about her marriage—she was very angry," Mary added as an afterthought. "Not that she showed her anger greatly, but I knew how angry she was. She went very pale and her eyes glittered."

"And what did Rodric say to his father in reply?"

"There was a murmur which I couldn't hear well enough. Alice was talking of withdrawing from the room. Then I heard Godfather shout: 'I'll not tolerate that indeed! I'll disinherit any son of mine who works with that Frenchman Delancey! Why, we're still at war with France! It would be an act of treason and I would denounce any such traitor to the Watch at Rye, whether or not he were my son!' "

"Did you hear any more?"

"Only the merest fragment of conversation. Alice was virtually pulling me from the room. Godfather bellowed: 'The devil with scandal! There are some matters which cannot be condoned no matter how much scandal they may cause. To masquerade as a highwayman and play schoolboy pranks is one matter; to treat with one's enemies in time of war is high treason!' And Rodric began: 'Papa, please listen to me—' Then I heard nothing further for we were outside in the hall and Alice had closed the door."

"What happened then? You went to the drawing room, didn't you, until you heard Esther's screams when she found Mr. Brandson dead?"

But she was frightened now. She licked her lips again. "Alice went to the nursery," she said at last. "I—I was anxious to talk to Rodric . . . After a moment or two I went downstairs again to the hall."

"But didn't you tell anyone this before?"

"No, no, I—well it was not important . . . I only wanted to see him on a personal matter . . . I reached the hall, and Rodric came out of the library. He looked very agitated. I called but he didn't stop so I ran after him. He went to the stables. Ned was there. One of the scullery maids . . . was there too. They had been sitting in the straw, for I remember Ned dusting his breeches as he stood up. Rodric told him to saddle his horse. Ned said why should he, he wasn't a groom. Rodric suddenly lost his temper, and began to shout at him . . . It—it was rather distressing . . . I went back to the house without making any further attempt to speak to Rodric, and returned to the drawing room."

"But didn't Ned say afterwards that he had seen you at the stables?"

"He didn't see me. Rodric began quarreling with him while I was still outside, and I didn't venture past the door. Nobody knew that I had left the drawing room save Rodric, and Rodric—" She checked herself.

"What?"

"Nothing." She turned to me earnestly. "You won't tell anyone, will you? You won't say I left the drawing room and ran after Rodric to the stables?"

"Well, no," I said bewildered. "Of course not. But—"

"It was a personal matter," she rushed on awkwardly.

"A matter purely concerning Rodric and myself. I didn't want anyone else to know I spent that afternoon trying to see Rodric alone." And an odd look of suppressed excitement flashed across her face for a moment to bewilder me still further.

"Oh," I said blankly.

There was a silence.

"What was Ned's relationship with his father?" I said suddenly. "Did Mr. Brandson never think of leaving the estate to Ned?"

"Oh no," she said at once. "There was no question of that."

"But why? I don't understand."

She flushed again and shifted from one foot to the other, the picture of embarrassment.

"I didn't understand either," she said, "for a long time. Then I overheard—" She stopped.

"Yes?"

"Ned wasn't Godfather's son," she said. "Godfather let him bear the name of Brandson only in order to avoid scandal, but Ned wasn't his son at all."

I went downstairs, my redingote draped around my shoulders, and the footman in the hall bowed and wished me good-day. When he saw I intended to leave the house by the front entrance, he opened the door for me and bowed again as I stepped out into the porch. Before me the ground sloped sharply to meet the level of the Marsh. Trees grew on the rise on which the house was built, but none grew on a high enough level to obscure the wide vistas visible on all sides, and to the south I could see the sun as it glinted on the roofs of Rye and Winchelsea and cast a brilliant sheen over the blue band of the sea; to the west was a glimpse of cultivated land; to the east stood the dots of grazing sheep white-gray against the green of the Marsh. Stepping down from the porch to the drive, I walked around the side of the house and found myself facing the stables. Between the stables and the house was a paved yard; a housemaid, engaged in hanging out the washing on a clothes' line, caught sight of me, dropped her basket of pegs and curtsied in confusion.

I smiled, bent my head slightly in acknowledgement and walked on. Perhaps after all it was not so oppressive to be the mistress of a large house.

I could hear the sound of voices from the stables as I approached, yet due to the way the building was constructed I could see no one within till I reached the doorway. Even then they did not notice me, and I saw at once how easy it would have been for Mary to have arrived on the threshold and withdrawn to eavesdrop without being seen.

I went forward into the stables.

They saw me then soon enough.

The two raw tousle-headed stable-lads fell silent and Ned picked himself up from the pile of straw which lay in one corner and flicked the dust from his breeches.

"Good afternoon," he said, looking a little surprised that I should venture into such a place. "I thought you were sick in bed."

"I thought you were out riding."

He laughed. "I've just come back."

"And I have just left my room."

We both laughed then. After a moment's hesitation he moved forward awkwardly and the stable-lads drew back and turned to attend their duties.

"I would offer to show you the garden," he said, "except we have very little garden to speak of. Behind the house, the land falls sheer to the Marsh. There's only a seat from where one can gaze north and on a fine day perhaps glimpse the spires of Canterbury."

"Is it fine enough today?"

"We could find out, if you wish." He led the way outside even before I could draw breath to assent, and I followed him into the yard beyond.

In fact there was more of a garden behind the house than he had led me to suppose. We passed an orangery and an artificial pool and a walled kitchen garden, and at length reached the view he had mentioned. It was indeed, a fine sight, for I could see to the edge of the Marsh and, it seemed, far north into the more diverse countryside of Kent.

We sat down on the wooden seat together while I surveyed the view.

"I see no sign of Canterbury," I remarked presently.

"You never will," he said. "I only said that to coax you to come here. I wanted to tell you how grateful I was to you for speaking to George as you did last night. If I didn't seem grateful then it was only because I was too upset to remember my manners."

"Please—"

"George and I don't get along as brothers should," he said. "We never have and we never will. I don't want to lie to you about it and feed you honeyed words, just because he's your husband. I think he's a scheming foreigner and he thinks I'm a good-for-nothing bastard, and there's no love lost between us."

I was entertained in spite of myself. "And is it true?" I said amused. "Are you a good-for-nothing bastard?"

He looked at me askance with his slanting black eyes

which were so like his mother's. "Perhaps!" His glance
became watchful.

"You're very enlightened," he said, "for a lady."

"In what way?"

"Most ladies seventeen years old could not bring themselves to say a word like that. As like as not they wouldn't
know the meaning of it in the first place."

"I've heard it used often enough," I said.

We looked at one another. He was very still.

"Perhaps it's different in London," he said after a
while. "Perhaps it's different there."

"I don't think so." And then I told him.

He was amazed. After a while he said: "Does anyone
know?"

"Only Axel."

"He knew when he married you?"

"Certainly."

"But you're such a lady!" he said in wonderment. "No
one would ever guess."

"Are all bastards supposed to walk around carrying a
little plaque which announces their unfortunate birth to
the world?"

He flung back his head and laughed. "I suppose not!"
He was serious again. "But someone must have cared for
you—spent money on your education . . ."

I told him about my parents. It was strangely comforting to talk to someone about them. I mentioned my education in Cheltenham, described our house in town, told
him about Alexander. When I stopped at last I felt more
peaceful than I had felt since my arrival at Haraldsdyke,
or indeed since my wedding day a week ago.

"You were fortunate," he said when I had finished, and
he didn't sound bitter. "You lived just as any legitimate

child would have lived. Your mother and father loved each other and loved you enough to take care of you. You were never threatened by your illegitimacy until they died."

"I—suppose not."

"Nobody cared for me like that," he said. "And I never knew what was wrong. I used to think it was because I was ugly or stupid, or because I was the youngest and my mother hadn't wanted another pregnancy. I was brought up by a succession of nursemaids and then sent to the grammar school at Rye. Rodric and Vere had private tutors, but that was considered a wasted expense where I was concerned. My—father seldom troubled to speak to me and my mother never once came to the nursery to see me. It was unfair that no one ever told me why I was ignored so much; it would have been easier if I'd known."

"But when did you find out?"

"When?" He looked straight ahead across the Marsh to Kent and his body was tensed and still. Then: "Last year," he said. "On Christmas Eve. Rodric told me on the day he died that I was a bastard."

There were clouds gathering in the west. A scudding wind ruffled my hair and made me draw the folds of the redingote more closely around my body.

"You're cold?" said Ned. "Perhaps you would prefer to go indoors. It's late in the year to sit outside."

"No, I'm warm enough for the moment." I waited, half-hoping he would tell me more without my asking further questions, but when he was silent, I said tentatively: "Why did Rodric tell you then?"

He shrugged and then shivered suddenly as if in revulsion. "We were quarreling."

The breeze whispered again over the Marsh. Far away in the west I saw the landscape begin to blur beneath the dark clouds.

"I never quarreled with Rodric," he said. "I thought too highly of him. But that afternoon he was in an ugly temper, I'd never seen him so angry before. I was in the stables talking to one of the girls from the kitchens and he came in and shouted for me to saddle his horse. I said, half-joking: 'Who do you mistake me for—a stable-lad? Do it yourself!' And before I could even draw breath to laugh he turned around and shouted: 'You damned bastard, don't you ever do what anyone tells you? My God, as if I haven't had enough troubles today, with my father roaring and ranting like a madman and Alice tempting Vere to have a fight with me, and that wretched Mary running after me and pestering me to read her cursed love sonnets! And to crown a disastrous day, you have to practice your high-and-mighty bastard's bad manners at my expense!'

"I was so stupefied by this attack that I said the first thing that came into my head. 'You'd better not call me bastard again,' I shouted back at him, 'or I'll knock you off that fine horse of yours!' I was really hurt that he should speak to me like that. Rodric and I never quarreled. Never. He had never abused me before . . .

"He said without looking at me: 'Well, you're no more than a bastard, are you? Don't you even know who you are by this time?' And as I stared at him, he said: 'Why do you suppose Papa never troubled to give you a private education?'

"He had the saddle in his hands and was saddling the horse himself as he spoke. It was like some horrible dream. I went on staring at him, and then I turned to the

scullery girl and said: 'You'd better get back to the kitchens. Cook will be looking for you.' I only knew that I
wanted to be rid of her, that I didn't want her to hear any
more.

" 'I don't understand you,' I said to Rodric. 'I don't
know what you mean.'

" 'Then ask Papa to explain to you,' he said, 'for Lord
knows I haven't the time. Or ask Mama who your father
was—if she can remember.'

"He was leading the horse out of the stable. I was so
numbed that I could hardly move. I managed to stammer: 'You've no right to say such a thing about Mama!
You're her favorite—how dare you talk of her like that?'

" 'Because I'm not afraid of the truth,' he said, mounting his horse without a backward glance. 'And I know too
damned well that Papa hasn't spoken two dozen words to
Mama in twenty years and has slept in a separate bedroom since before you were born. You're so busy con-
sorting with stable-lads and scullery maids that you
haven't seen enough of either Mama or Papa to realize
they're married in name only. Why do you suppose Papa
keeps a mistress at Hastings and Mama has discreet affairs with any man she can contrive to seduce?'

"Even speech was impossible now. I could only stand
in the doorway and lean against the post and watch the
world crumble before my eyes.

"He was in the saddle. I remember that moment so
well. The sun was shining down on him and his eyes were
very blue. 'To hell with the lot of you,' he said, 'I'm going
to ride until I'm too weary to care. To hell with you all.'
And he rode off down the hill to the Marsh and the sun
went in and I felt the rain sting my cheek. The mist blew
in from the sea soon afterwards and the sun was gone."

There was a silence. To the west the Marsh was now indistinct and the clouds stretched to the blurred horizon. I was going to speak, but he spoke first, his eyes watching some distant point on the Marsh as if he were seeing other scenes long ago.

"I watched him go," he said. "I watched him until he was out of sight. Afterwards I thought how unfair it was that we parted in such anger, but at that moment I was aware of nothing at all, only a dreadful emptiness. Afterwards I went back into the stable and flung myself down on the straw again. I didn't even cry. That came later. After a time I thought: 'I must find Papa and ask him for the truth.' So I left the stables and went back into the house.

"There was no footman in the hall. I went to the library and knocked on the door but there was no reply, so I went upstairs to Papa's rooms. He wasn't there. Then I thought: 'I'll find Mama and speak to her.'

"At first I thought she wasn't in her rooms either. I went into the boudoir but that was empty and then when I was turning to leave I heard the murmur of voices from the bedroom beyond."

I turned my head sharply to look at him, but he was still staring out across the Marsh, his elbows on his knees, his fists clenched.

"I knew then it was all true," he said at last. "I didn't need to be convinced further. She was with some man. The very discovery seemed instantly to confirm everything Rodric had said."

I was perfectly still. "Who was the man with her?" said my voice with polite interest. "You're sure it wasn't your father?"

"Yes."

"How can you be sure?"

He did not answer directly. Then he bent down and began to tug up the grass at his feet as though some form of action however mild would excuse him from replying.

"Ned?" I was still very polite.

"I heard his steps crossing to open the door into the boudoir," he said in a muffled voice. "There wasn't time for me to escape so I hid behind the Chinese screen in one corner of the room. He came out a second later and she followed him."

"Who was he?"

"I'll not tell you."

I grabbed his wrist and jerked him as hard as I could so that he spun around to face me. I was trembling in every limb now no matter how hard I tried to conceal it.

"Was it Axel?"

"I'll not tell you."

"It must have been! There was no other man in the house who was not related to her."

"There were servants."

"Ned!"

"I'll not tell you," he said stubbornly. "I've never told anyone before and I'm not telling you."

"You didn't tell the coroner at the inquest?"

"No, why should I have done? He would have wanted to know why I went in search of my mother in the first place, and I had no intention of repeating to the coroner and half the population of Rye what Rodric had told me."

I stared at him.

"I wish I had never mentioned it," he said sullenly. "I don't know why I did. You made me forget to guard my tongue."

"Did they discover you in the boudoir?" I demanded, ignoring this. "Did they see you?"

"No, thank the Lord. It was lucky the screen was there, for there was nowhere else I could have hidden."

"What did they say to each other?"

"She said 'I must go and see if anything can be done.' And the man said: 'I'll come downstairs with you.' They went out of the room and I heard her say to him in the passage: 'What do you suppose he wanted?' And he said after a moment: 'Perhaps to ask you if you knew about the French contraband he found in the barn below the thirty-acre field. He told me two days ago he was watching the barn to catch whoever was in league with Delancey, but when I told him to go straight to the Revenue Men he wouldn't, too afraid it might be one of Rodric's foolish pranks again, I suppose.' Then they turned the corner to the landing, and I didn't hear any more."

"And the next moment you heard Esther's screams when she discovered Mr. Brandson dead?"

"No," he said. "It was about ten minutes later."

"Ten minutes! But it couldn't have taken her that long to reach the library!"

"Then maybe it took her ten minutes to draw breath to scream," he said, "for I didn't hear the screams till some time later. I left the boudoir as quickly as I could and went to my own room and lay on my bed thinking. I must have lain there at least ten minutes."

"How very curious."

"When I heard her screams I went to the head of the staircase. George and Mary were in the hall with my mother and Alice was descending the staircase ahead of me. I ran downstairs. One of the footmen was wandering around white as parchment and saying 'No one left the li-

brary save Mr. Rodric.' A great deal *he* knew about *that!*
He hadn't even been there when I had knocked on the library door."

"What did you do?"

"I went into the library. The others were too busy
soothing Mama's hysterics. Papa was sprawled across the
floor and Rodric's gun lay beside him, the butt smeared
with blood. Rodric had been out shooting with George
that morning. I was stunned enough already and when I
saw the scene in the library it made no impression on me
at all at first. And then gradually I felt full of panic and a
longing to escape so I ran back to my room, locked the
door and broke down completely. I lay on my bed and
sobbed till I had no strength to do anything except fall
asleep. It was like being in a nightmare unable to wake."

"When did you hear of Rodric's death?"

"Later that evening when George returned. Mary came
knocking at my door. Have you talked much to Mary? If
you have, you'll realize she was infatuated with Rodric
and used to imagine herself affianced to him and other
such nonsense. Rodric tried to be patient with her out of
kindness, but I fancy she irritated him more often than
not. But, poor girl, she was beside herself with grief then
and came to me because she knew how fond of him I was
too. As soon as she told me I went downstairs.

"George was in the saloon with Vere, Alice and Mama.
He was soaked to the skin and looked more shaken than I
have ever seen him. I said: 'How did he die?' And George
said: 'He must have fallen from his horse. There was a
dyke, a tract of bog, and I found his hat nearby and his
horse wandering further on. He must have drowned in the
Marsh.' And Vere said: 'Perhaps he was overcome with
remorse.' And Alice said: 'God forgive him.'

"That was what everyone said after the inquest. 'God forgive him,' everyone kept saying. 'God forgive him.' It was horrible! He was branded as a murderer without so much as a fair trial!"

Close at hand long fingers of white mist wreathed the landscape so that the Marsh seemed eerie, adrift in some strange twilight. I shivered.

"You're cold now," said Ned. "We'd better go in."

I stood up without argument, and we walked together in silence through the garden to the house. I felt so numbed that I hardly noticed that it was beginning to rain.

"Perhaps the greatest shock of all came when Mr. Sherman read the will," Ned said. "We all thought that Haraldsdyke had been left to Rodric with a suitable bequest to Vere. We had no idea Papa had made the other will the day before he died."

"Yes," I said. "Axel told me it was a matter of embarrassment to him."

"Embarrassment!" scoffed Ned. "He wasn't embarrassed! I swore he knew all along about the new will! I was so angry that Vere, who's always worked so hard for Haraldsdyke, should have inherited nothing, that I lost my temper when I should have guarded my tongue. George was having a word with me in private before he departed for Vienna—he wanted to tell me he would arrange for me to have an income of thirty pounds a year, but he made it sound as if he were bestowing a great favor on me. And suddenly I thought how generous Rodric had always been with his money and that this man was now sitting in Rodric's place and dealing with money that should have belonged to Rodric himself.

" 'I think I should have fifty pounds per annum,' I said. 'You can afford to be generous. You took Haraldsdyke from Papa after his death and you took his wife before his death—' " He stopped dead in his tracks.

It was raining steadily now. The mist was falling between us. Everywhere was very quiet.

"So it *was* Axel whom you found with Esther," I heard myself say calmly from a long way away.

He looked as if he could have bitten out his tongue. "Yes," he said at last, face flushed with embarrassment. "It was. But I never told him how I had seen him come out of Mama's bedroom that day. For God's sake never, never tell him that."

"Why? Are you so afraid of him?"

"I—" The words seemed to stick in his throat.

"You think Axel killed his father, don't you? That Rodric was innocent?"

"I—I've no proof . . . only that they went downstairs together to the library and that Mama didn't scream till fully ten minutes later. Perhaps Papa had found out they were deceiving him, perhaps there was yet another quarrel in the library after Rodric left . . ."

"But surely Mr. Brandson was already dead? You said that after lingering a while in the stables you returned to the hall, knocked on the library door, and received no reply—"

"There are a dozen other explanations for that. He may have stepped out on to the terrace for a moment—or next door into the saloon—or he may not have heard me—or he may even have been asleep. He did sleep there sometimes. I've no proof that he was dead then, just as I've no proof that he quarreled with George and that

George killed him. But I think Rodric was innocent. I shall always think that. I'll never believe that Rodric killed Papa."

We reached a side-door which led into the saloon from the terrace, and he opened it for me. The saloon was empty. "What did Axel say," I said abruptly, "when you revealed to him that you knew about his relationship with Esther?"

"He asked me to explain myself. I merely shrugged and said: 'I saw you once with her.' I pretended to be very casual. Then I said as an afterthought: 'I wonder what the coroner would have thought at the inquest if he knew you had been having an affair with your step-mother besides having that will made in your favor?'"

I drew a deep breath. "What did he say?"

"He was very still. Then gradually he went white with rage. After a moment he said: 'If you so much as attempt to create a scandal for your mother after she has endured so much shock and suffering, I swear I'll break every bone in your body.' At least, he spoke in rougher language than those words, and called me a bastard—and other names as well. How I hated him at that moment! Presently I said: 'I've no intention of making a scandal, but I would like that fifty pounds a year which I mentioned just now.' "

"And what happened?" I said blankly. "Did he agree to the sum you wanted?"

"Oh yes," said Ned. "He agreed."

Four

AXEL AND VERE were not at Haraldsdyke for dinner. After the meal I was obliged to sit for a while in the drawing room with Esther and Mary while Alice went to the nursery, but at last I was able to make my excuses and escape. Dusk was already falling as I reached our sitting room upstairs; I lit two candles, carried them to the secretaire by the window and sat down. Pen and ink were quickly found, but there was no paper. I thought suddenly of the huge desk in Rodric's room. Surely there would be paper in one of the drawers...

I stood up, took one of the candles and went out into the passage. No one was about. I had some trouble finding Rodric's room again, but eventually I remembered my way and discovered a plentiful supply of the writing paper I needed. It was quite dark now. Back in my own rooms again, I sat down with a strange feeling of relief, picked up the pen and began to write to Alexander.

Time was short; at any moment Axel might return from Rye. My pen scratched rapidly across the paper, dropped a blob of ink and scratched on without pausing. The entire appearance of the letter would have horrified old Miss Shearing at my academy in Cheltenham. Miss Shearing and her environment all seemed very far away indeed.

"I hope you are well at school," I scribbled. "I wish it were the end of term, for I miss you even more than usual." I paused, mindful that I must take great care not to say too much. "Haraldsdyke is a most unusual house," I wrote quickly after a moment, "and the family have been most civil and kind. You would like it here because you could ride every day, if you wished, and there's plenty of game for shooting on the Marsh. Is it not possible that you could leave before term's end? Christmas is still several weeks away and it seems such a long time to wait till I see you again. I have so much to tell you, more than can ever be put in a mere letter . . ." Careful. I gnawed the end of the quill, absorbed in my task, oblivious to everything around me. I must, I thought, be a little more specific or the entire point of the letter would be lost. Alexander was not quick to grasp hints and allusions. "You will not credit this," I resumed presently, "but it turns out that Mr. Robert Brandson, Axel's father, did not die a natural death at all, as we were led to suppose, and was in fact the victim of a murderous attack last Christmas Eve. It was presumed by the Coroner's Jury that the perpetrator of the deed was Axel's half-brother, Mr. Rodric Brandson, but as he died but a few hours after his father as the result of an accident, he was never able to defend himself against such a charge of murder. Even though it is generally accepted that he was guilty, there are nonetheless some who say . . ."

There was a sound from behind me.

I spun around, and the pen spluttered on the paper beneath the convulsive start of my hand.

"You should have another candle," said Axel, "lest you strain your eyes in such a dim light."

I had never even heard him enter the room. Such was my paralysis of surprise that I could do nothing except stare at him and hope the light was dim enough to hide the pallor of my face and the expression in my eyes.

"Did I startle you?" he said. "I'm sorry." He was very close to me now, and as he stooped to kiss me he saw the letter and I instinctively turned it face downwards on the blotter.

"I had inkspots all over the paper," I said, speaking the first thought to enter my head. "If it were to anyone else but to Alexander I would write the letter afresh on a clean piece of paper, but he won't mind my untidiness."

"It was thoughtful of you to write so soon after your arrival." His fingers were against my cheek, the long cool fingers which I now knew so well. He was gently forcing me to look at him.

"How did you fare in Rye?" I said instantly, looking him straight in the eyes.

"Well enough. Aren't you going to give me a kiss?"

"Of course," I said, cool as spring water, and rose to my feet as I raised my face to his.

He slid his arms around my waist and kissed me on the mouth with an intimacy which was as unexpected as it was unwelcome.

"You have no idea how good it is," he said, "to ride

home through the foggy dusk of a November evening and then find you here, looking as you look now . . . Are you feeling better?"

"Yes, thank you," I said, and then added, lest he should be harboring any ideas to the contrary, "but I shall be a trifle delicate for two or three days yet."

"You must take care of yourself." He released me and turned aside abruptly. I saw his glance rest again on the letter, and my heart began to bump uncomfortably once more. "I shall be riding to Rye again tomorrow," he said. "I'll take your letter with me. There's a mail-coach which leaves tomorrow at noon for Tunbridge Wells and London, and I can arrange with the coachman to see that the letter is safely sent from London to Harrow."

"Please, I wouldn't want it to inconvenience you."

"There would be no inconvenience. If you haven't yet finished the letter, perhaps you could add a sentence giving my regards to Alexander and saying that we look forward to seeing him at Christmas."

What else was there to say? I returned to my writing, and presently he rang for his valet and I heard him telling the man to arrange for a light meal to be served in our apartments.

"Will you sup with me?" he asked. "Or would you prefer to eat with the others? I'm hungry and tired and have no wish to join them."

"I'm not hungry at present," I said. "It's not so long since I dined. I'll wait and then drink tea with the others, with your permission."

I re-wrote the letter to Alexander, carefully omitting any reference to the fact that Rodric's guilt was doubted in any way. From the subject of the murder, I then described Haraldsdyke in minute detail and mentioned each of the family by name. Finally I carefully added Axel's message and wrote below it: "Do come as soon as you can!" before signing my name.

By the time I laid down my pen, he was eating his supper at the table by the window.

"I would like to see more of Rye," I said on an impulse. "Would it be possible for me to travel with you tomorrow?"

"In your present state of health?"

"I—I wasn't thinking of riding, I thought perhaps the carriage."

"I think the journey would tire you all the same, and besides, I have business to conduct and wouldn't be able to attend to you. Another time, perhaps."

"Perhaps Ned would come with me if you were too busy."

He gave me a hard look. "Ned?"

"I—was talking to him today . . . I found him pleasant enough. I thought that perhaps . . ."

"You will not," said Axel distinctly, "travel to Rye with Ned."

"Very well. As you wish."

"You would be best advised to spend the day with Alice and learn more about your household. No doubt there will be callers too who wish to present themselves and you should be there to receive them."

"Yes," I said. I glanced at the clock on the mantelpiece above the fireplace. "Will you excuse me, Axel, if I leave you now? I think perhaps tea will be ready soon, and I'm hungrier now than I was earlier."

He gave his permission. Taking a candle I went out into the corridor, and had just reached the landing when I remembered with horror that I had not destroyed my original letter to Alexander but had left it carelessly folded on the secretaire with my completed letter.

I turned at once and ran back down the passage. I was already in the room when I remembered I had not even paused to invent an excuse for my return.

Luckily I had no need of one; Axel had already gone into the bedroom beyond. Moving hastily across to the secretaire I snatched up the original letter and cast it into the midst of the fire. It was only as I stood watching it burn that it occurred to me to wonder if the folded note-paper had been exactly as I had left it on the secretaire . . .

The next morning was dull and tedious. Knowing that when Axel returned from Rye he would be sure to ask me how I had spent the day, I asked Alice to show me the kitchens and her household affairs. Then the rector's wife and sister called again, and I had to be civil and welcoming to them in an attempt to create a good impression. When they had gone, Alice took me to the nursery to show me her children, and again I had to be careful to say exactly the right words and choose appropriately admiring remarks. Stephen, the eldest, was a quiet shy child with fair hair and green eyes, but Clarissa, a year younger, was already as big as he was and much more boisterous. The youngest, Robert, had an aggressive chin which looked odd on so young a child, and a loud voice which he used with deafening effect.

"The little love," said Alice fondly, picking him up, and he was instantly quiet and well-behaved.

Seeing her with the children reminded me of my fear of pregnancy, and I was glad when I had the chance to escape to my rooms at last. But I could not stay in the rooms long; I was restless and had no wish at all to sit and think heaven knows what manner of thoughts, and soon I was donning my pelisse and some warm boots and slipping downstairs with the idea of walking in the garden. I had hardly taken a step outside when Ned came around the corner of the house and nearly bumped into me.

We laughed; he apologized and I said it was nothing. Presently I asked him where he was going.

"To Haraldsford, the nearest village," he said. "I promised Alice I would take a ham and some pies to her mother. Why don't you come with me? It's not far—only a mile."

"Will we be back in time for dinner?"

"Why, yes—easily. We'll be gone less than an hour all told."

I was immensely curious to see Alice's mother, the witch.

"Very well, I'll come," I said, "only it must be a secret. I am supposed to spend all day at the house learning about the household affairs of Haraldsdyke."

He smiled, his teeth white and even, his black eyes sparkling. "Your secret's safe with me."

So we set off together for the village, and immediately the house was behind us I was conscious of relief and felt almost light-hearted.

We were soon there. The road was built up above the level of the land, which seemed curious to me, but around the village the level rose to meet the road. It was a very small place; there was a round Saxon church with a Norman tower attached, several cottages and an inn called "The Black Ram." Alice's mother lived in a tiny hovel apart from the others on the edge of the village; a nanny-goat grazed by the door and two hens peered out of the open doorway.

"She's a witch, I believe," I said casually to Ned as we drew nearer, but Ned only laughed.

"So they say—just because she knows a few old potions and a spell or two! I'll believe she's a witch the day I see her ride a broomstick, and not till then."

I was disappointed. I was even more disappointed when I saw that Alice's mother Dame Joan was not a hump-backed evil creature clad in black rags, but a broad strong country woman with an arrogant nose, a powerful voice and strange light eyes of no particular color but full of grays and greens and blue flecks.

"Good-day, Dame Joan," said Ned briskly. "Alice sent me with some gifts for you. I hope you're well and in good health."

She shot him a sharp look and then glanced at me. "You'll be the foreigner's wife," she said at once.

I suppose it was an obvious enough deduction, but I was childishly thrilled at the confident way she announced my identity.

"Yes indeed," said Ned, winking at me. "Mrs. George Brandson."

I smiled at her and said "good-day" but she merely said: "You're an insolent rascal, boy. I saw you twist your face to mock me."

I was alarmed, thinking he had offended her, but he merely laughed. "Have you eyes in the back of your head, then, Dame Joan?" he said amused. "I was standing behind you—how could you see what I was doing?"

"I've ways," she said darkly. "You'd best be careful or next time you go changing the shapes of new scullery maids I'll not be so free and easy with my remedies."

But Ned refused to be either embarrassed or deflated. "Dame Joan is an authority on all manner of things connected with fertility," he said to me frankly with his careless smile. "If you're not pregnant and want to be so, she gives you a potion. If you're pregnant and don't want to be so she gives you another potion. If you're not pregnant and don't want to be so—"

"Young rascal," said Dame Joan. "Talking before a lady like that. The foreigner would beat you sore if he heard you."

There was something uncanny about her perception of Axel's attitude to Ned. Even Ned himself was caught unawares; I saw the smile vanish from his face for a moment and then he was laughing again, refusing to be perturbed.

"Dame Joan knows there's no love lost between me and George," he said lightly. "Well, we must be on our way home for dinner. Good-day to you, Dame Joan, and I hope you enjoy the ham and the pies."

But as we walked away from the village he said without looking at me: "I'm sorry if I spoke too bluntly. I had no wish to offend you."

"There was no offense," I said truthfully. "My father was always very frank in his conversation and didn't care a whit how outspoken he was."

He smiled, obviously relieved. Presently he said: "I can't think how you'll settle at Haraldsdyke."

"Why do you say that?"

"Well! You're so—so alive, so . . ." He shrugged, at a loss for words. "You should be in a city," he said, "wearing beautiful clothes and jewelry and mingling with Society, not cut off here in the country with no one to impress save the local gentry and the merchants of the Cinque Ports! You'll be stifled, bored—"

"Nonsense!" I spoke all the more intensely because I was afraid there was an element of truth in what he said.

"But you're so alive!" he said. "So full of interest. So different from these country girls with their giggles and prudery and dreary conversation."

"You'd best stop this at once," I said, "or I shall become so vain that my head will be too swollen to permit me to walk through the doorway in Haraldsdyke." But I was pleased all the same.

Esther met us in the hall when we arrived back. I was half-afraid she had seen us walk up the drive together.

"Ah, there you are!" she said to me, and as I looked at her I thought instantly of her former relationship with Axel and had to repress my longing to rebuff her air of welcoming friendliness which I had never fully accepted as sincere. "We were wondering where you were, my dear," she said, and her dark eyes glanced from me to Ned and back to me again. "George is home from Rye, and asked to see you as soon as you returned."

Some instinct told me even before I entered the room that the interview which lay ahead of me would be unpleasant. Axel was in his dressing room; I heard him dismiss his valet as he heard me enter the apartments. The next moment he was entering the sitting room where I was waiting, and crossing the floor to greet me.

"Did you have a satisfactory day in Rye?" I asked, rather too quickly. "I'm glad you were able to be back for dinner today."

"I was surprised to find you absent on my arrival home," he said dryly, and gestured towards the hearth. "Let's sit down for a moment."

I settled myself on the edge of the high-backed fireside chair and folded my hands in my lap. My heart was bumping noisily; I tried to look cool and composed.

"Alice told me you spent some time with her this morning," he said. "I was glad to hear you'd taken my advice to heart."

I launched into a detailed account of the time I had spent with Alice. He listened intently. At last when I could think of nothing further to say he said: "After you left Alice I understand you went for a walk with Ned."

"Yes, to Haraldsford, to take some provisions to Alice's mother. But how did you—"

"Esther saw you leave."

There was a pause. I was suddenly very angry at the thought of Esther spying upon me, but I managed to control the impulse to put my thoughts into words.

"I see," I said.

"You remember that I had forbidden you to go to Rye in Ned's company."

"I remember."

"Surely you must have realized by now that I wish you to see as little of Ned as possible?"

"It had occurred to me."

"Yet you sought his company to walk to Haraldsford!"

"That was a mere chance." I explained what had happened. "I didn't think you would mind," I added, "or of course I wouldn't have gone."

"I mind very much you being seen alone in his company," Axel said sharply. "He has a bad reputation, particularly in regard to girls of your age, and he mixes with people with whom it would be ill-advised for you to associate yourself. You forget you're now mistress of

Haraldsdyke, not a mere schoolgirl whose behavior can be overlooked or excused."

"I am perfectly well aware that I am mistress of Haraldsdyke," I said icily. "What you seem to forget is that Ned is your half-brother and by normal social standards would be considered a fitting escort for me on a short country walk."

I was furiously angry, of course, or I would never have dared to speak to him in that manner. For a moment he seemed taken aback at my audacity for I saw his eyes widen slightly, and then he was himself again, very cool and remote.

"He's no kin of mine."

"So I've been told," I said cuttingly, "but as this isn't generally known it would make no difference to the fact that in the eyes of the world he would still be considered a suitable escort." And I stood up and moved swiftly next door into the bedroom, the tears stinging my eyes.

He followed me instantly and closed the door. "Listen to me," he said. "Be that as it may, I still have reasons of my own for not wishing you to associate with Ned. I must insist that you heed what I say and see as little of him as possible."

My tears by this time made speech impossible. I was hopelessly upset, wishing with all my heart that I could run to my mother for comfort, and the wish only served to remind me that she was dead and lost to me forever. Tears scalded my cheeks; I stared out of the window, my back to the stranger behind me, my whole will concentrating on the task of concealing my lack of self-control.

"Are you listening to what I'm saying?" said Axel sharply.

I bent my head in acknowledgement.

"Then I would like your promise that you will do as I tell you."

I tried to speak but could not. Seconds passed.

"I'm waiting, my dear."

Sobs trembled in my throat. Suddenly my shoulders were shaking. I closed my eyes in wretchedness, and then his hand was touching my shoulder and his voice said with unexpected gentleness: "Forgive me. I see I've been too harsh."

To my shame I let him press me to him and hide my face against his breast; his fingers stroked my hair.

"But you were outwardly so proud and independent!" he said regretfully. "I did not realize—"

I turned aside from him, my tears under control. "There was no question of you being too harsh," I said stonily. "I was suddenly reminded of my parents' death and was overcome with grief for a moment. I'm sorry to have made such an exhibition of my feelings before you. And now, if you will excuse me, I shall change and dress for dinner."

He bowed silently and after a moment withdrew to his dressing room once more. I waited for him to call for his valet, but he did not and the silence remained like a pall over the room.

I was still by the window some minutes later when he came back to talk to me.

I gave a start of surprise.

"I quite forgot to tell you," he said. "I have asked the Shermans to dine with us tomorrow. James Sherman, as you may remember, was my father's lawyer."

"Very well," I said, perhaps sounding more dignified

than I intended. "I'll see that the necessary arrangements are made to receive him. How many visitors will there be?"

"Five in all. Sherman himself, his wife and daughters, and his brother Charles."

"Five. Thank you."

A pause. The gulf yawned between us. Then:

"I have just one question to ask you about Ned," he said quietly, "and then we need make no further reference to the subject. Did he speak to you of Rodric?"

I stared. His face was watchful but I could not read the expression in his eyes.

"No," I said, and then realizing that this would seem unlikely I added: "At least, he merely mentioned him and said how fond of him he had been."

"I see."

"Why do you ask?" I said as he turned to go. "Is there some mystery about Rodric?"

"None that I know of," he said flatly, and withdrew without further comment to his dressing room.

Dinner was at four o'clock; outside dusk was falling and the rain came sweeping across the Marsh to dash itself against the window-panes. Axel and I entered the dining room to find Mary already seated in an unbecoming violet gown with puffed cap-sleeves which made her plump arms look even larger than they were. Ned came in a moment later; he was clean and tidy, and although Axel looked at him very hard it seemed he could find no fault with Ned's appearance tonight. Esther came in soon after Ned. She looked very handsome in black satin, the sombre shade of mourning suiting her much too well, the gown cut to compliment each line of her figure so that it was hard to believe she was old enough to be the mother of grown sons. She looked at me curiously, as if she were trying to perceive whether Axel had reprimanded me for walking to Haraldsford with Ned, and I was careful to smile with just the right degree of coldness so that she would realize I had survived her attempts at interference with ease and despised her for her prying into my personal affairs.

Vere and Alice came into the room to complete the gathering, I said grace as shortly as possible and we sat down to eat.

I soon noticed Vere's moroseness, but it took me till the second course to realize that he and Axel were not speaking to one another. In contrast Alice seemed untroubled and we talked together for a while of her mother. Mary as usual was too withdrawn to contribute much to the conversation and Ned seemed to have no other ambition than to eat his food as quickly and unobtrusively as possible. At the other end of the table, Axel and Esther maintained a formal conversation for a while, but in general it was a silent meal, and I was glad when it was over and it was time for the women to withdraw.

As we went upstairs to the drawing room I heard Esther say to Alice: "Has Vere quarreled with George?"

And Alice said: "There were difficulties today in Rye."

Further conversation on this topic was not possible between them as we reached the drawing room door a moment later.

After ten minutes I excused myself, saying I was tired after a long day, and in truth I did feel rather more weary than usual, probably on account of the strain of the morning spent with Alice while she had instructed me on household matters. In my rooms once more I summoned

Marie-Claire, made an elaborate toilette and was between
the sheets of the big double-bed by six o'clock.

At first I thought that sleep would come easily, but as
sometimes happens, although my limbs soon became
warm and relaxed my mind quickened and sharpened
until in the end even the physical peace began to ebb and
I tossed and turned restlessly. I was thinking of Axel's relationship with Esther still, examining the idea minutely
until there was not a single aspect which had escaped my
consideration. Esther was probably no more than twelve
years Axel's senior, possibly even less; she was good-
looking, worldly and shrewd, bored enough with her
empty marriage to take lovers when the opportunity
arose, sharp enough to see that her sophisticated step-son
with his cosmopolitan city background could prove a
welcome diversion.

And Axel, despite the respect he always claimed to
bear towards his father, had allowed himself to be diverted. Her maturity would have appealed to him, no doubt;
he would certainly belong to her generation more than to
mine.

I pictured his arrival at Haraldsdyke the previous
Christmas, the quick flare as the affair was set alight, the
holocaust of discovery. I could almost hear Robert
Brandson shout in the rich English voice I had never
heard: "I made a new will leaving all to you, but I shall
revoke it! I'll not leave you a penny of my money, not a
stone of Haraldsdyke!" And then afterwards Rodric
would have been the perfect scapegoat, all the more perfect since he had not been alive to declare his innocence.
Axel had ridden off after him into the mist and found
only his horse and hat among the marshes.

Or so Axel said.

I sat up, sweat on my forehead, my limbs trembling and fumbled for the sulphur and the match jar to light the lamp.

Of course, the affair was all over now; it had ended in disaster and Axel would be sharp enough to see that any hint that such a situation had ever existed must be suppressed. He would hardly be foolish enough to continue the affair now.

Unless he loved her. It was obvious he did not love me. He was fond enough of me to make a display of affection effortless, but there was no question of love. Why should there be? I had not loved him. It had been a marriage of convenience and would remain so. Why not? Who married for love nowadays anyway? Only fools. Or paupers. Or those born to good luck and happiness.

I slipped out of bed, my throat tight and aching, and drew on a warm woolen robe to protect me from the damp chill of the November night. In the room next door the fire had burned low, but I stirred the embers with the poker and threw on another lump of coal with the fireside tongs. For a long time I sat on the hearth and watched the leaping flames and wondered if I would still imagine such terrible scenes involving Axel if he loved me and I loved him in return. Perhaps if I knew he loved me I would not mind whatever had happened in the past. Perhaps I would even be sorry for Esther, poor Esther whose youth was gone and who would soon lose much of the magnetism on which she relied to escape from the hideous boredom of widowhood in the country. Nothing would matter so much if Axel loved me a little, if I did not feel so lost and adrift and alone . . .

I stood up, went out into the corridor, moved to the head of the stairs. Voices were still coming from the

drawing room so I assumed that no one else had yet retired, but there were no sounds of masculine voices either,
which seemed to indicate that the men were still in the
dining room.

I padded aimlessly downstairs to the deserted hall and
wandered into the saloon next to the library in which
Robert Brandson had met his death nearly a year ago.
Candles were alight on the table; a fire was burning in the
grate and the room was warm; when I heard the voices
from the room next door a second later, I paused, knowing I should not listen but aware only of my curiousity.
Finally the hesitation passed and the shame was overcome; softly closing the door of the saloon behind me I
tip-toed over to the window and sat on the window-seat
which lay behind the long curtains and close to the communicating door between the two rooms. The door, of
course, was closed, but evidently it fitted badly, for the
conversation was audible and I could understand then
how easily Alice and Mary had heard nearly every word
of the quarrel between Rodric and his father which had
taken place last Christmas Eve.

"God damn you," said Vere in a soft distinct voice.
"God damn you, George Brandson."

"You may seek my damnation as often as you wish,"
said Axel, cool as ice, the faint flavor of contempt lingering in each syllable. "You may invoke the Deity from this
hour to eternity, but it won't alter my decision. When I
left here after Papa's death it was arranged with the trustees of his will that you were to have enough power to administer Haraldsdyke and the estate for one year or for
such time as elapsed before I fulfilled the conditions of
my inheritance. You've been in control here for nearly a

year. And what's happened? You've incurred debts which
you were not legally entitled to incur, you've lost money
hand over fist and you've indulged in some agricultural
experiments which I think even the most enlightened
agrarian would call hazardous in the extreme. The trustees, as we saw today, are seriously embarrassed and I
don't blame them. I would be too if I were in their position and had to render accounts relating to the past financial year at Haraldsdyke. I had hoped to be able to
rely on you heavily when it came to administering the estate, but now I see I shall have to revise my ideas. It's
obvious you have no more grasp of finance than Rodric
had, and Lord knows that was little enough."

"Don't you compare me with Rodric!" Vere's quiet
voice rose in fury. "My God, I suffered enough from
comparisons while he was alive to endure listening to
more of them now he's dead! It was always the same, always—I was the only one who really cared for Haraldsdyke and wanted to improve the land, yet what chance
did I ever have to prove myself when Papa was too pig-
headed to permit any changes? He never listened to me!
Nobody ever listened to me! Everything was Rodric, Rodric, Rodric—and what did Rodric ever do except squander
his opportunities and spend money like water on his damn-
fool escapades? But Rodric was precious, Rodric was
sacred! Papa listened to Rodric, even when he never had
time to listen to me—condoned Rodric's affairs but
wouldn't forgive me for my marriage—showered Rodric
with money for his pleasures, but made me beg for any
money to spend on Haraldsdyke."

"I'm not in the least interested," Axel interrupted acidly, "in your past grievances and grudges concerning Rod-

ric. What I'm concerned about is the fact that over the
past year you've lost a considerable amount of my
money."

"It can be repaid. A great deal of it is merely a tempo-
rary loss which will be made good next year. I still main-
tain that my schemes are worthy of consideration."

"Then I'm afraid I am completely unable to agree with
you."

"In God's name!" shouted Vere so loudly that I
thought his cry must have resounded throughout the
house. "Why do I always have to beg for what I want?
I'm sick to death of begging! If I had any money of my
own I swear I would wash my hands of you all and buy
my own land and build my own farm!"

"I'm only sorry Papa did not provide for you in his
will, but he evidently had his reasons . . ."

"I don't want your sympathy! The money would have
come to me if Papa hadn't made the will in your favor
without anyone knowing he was going to cut Rodric out
of any share of the inheritance, the money was to come to
me."

"Please," said Axel, "let's be realistic and not speculate
about what might or might not have taken place if circumstances had been different. The money is mine and
Haraldsdyke is mine, but I'm willing enough to share it
with you to some extent and let you continue to administer
the estate as you think best. However, obviously if any
liberality is going to result in heavy financial loss—"

"You surely can't judge me on the results of a year's
bad luck!"

"I think there's rather more than bad luck involved."

"And what do you know about the estate anyway?
How can you tell? I've slaved and toiled and worked long

hours for Haraldsdyke. I love it better than any place on earth! And now you come along and try to tell me I've deliberately misappropriated your money—"

"Nonsense. All I'm saying is that I'm not in favor of any further agricultural experimentation for at least three years and won't advance you large sums of money to apply to schemes which are as yet untried and dangerous."

"And who are you to judge? What do you know of agriculture anyway? Who are you to make decisions which may affect the whole future of Haraldsdyke?"

"My dear Vere," said Axel, half-amused, half-exasperated. "Haraldsdyke *is* mine! And it *is* my money! I think I'm entitled to some say in the matter."

"Yes!" cried Vere, "Haraldsdyke is yours and the money is yours because, luckily for you, Papa made a will in your favor in a fit of mental aberration and then conveniently died before he could change it!"

There was a short tingling silence. Then Axel said quietly: "Precisely what are you suggesting?"

"Why, nothing! Merely that it was fortunate for you that Papa died when he did—and that Rodric died before he could answer his accusers!"

"Are you by any conceivable chance trying to imply that . . ."

"I mean what I say, not a word more and not a word less!"

"Then you'd best be extraordinarily careful, hadn't you, Vere, because like any other gentleman I'm exceedingly averse to being slandered and am—fortunately—in a position to retaliate very seriously indeed."

The silence flared, lengthened, became unbearable. Then:

"Just remember, won't you," said Axel, the door to the hall clicking as he opened it, "that you and your family live here for as long as I wish—and not a second longer."

The door snapped shut; his footsteps crossed the hall to the stairs and were soon inaudible. In the heavy silence that followed I was just about to push back the curtains and leave the window-seat when the communicating door from the library burst open and Vere came into the room.

He could not see me; the long curtains before the window hid me from view, and as he slammed the door shut behind him the curtains trembled in the draft of air. I found a chink in the curtains, and not daring to move or display myself I remained where I was, frozen into immobility as I watched him.

He had taken the wine decanter and was pouring himself a drink. A minute later, the glass empty, he poured himself a second measure and then slumped into a hearthside chair and put his head in his hands. I waited, scarcely daring to breathe, hoping he would go, but he remained motionless by the fire. I began to worry; how long would he stay there? If Axel had gone to our rooms he would discover I was missing and wonder why I had not returned.

He had just finished his second glass of wine and was to my despair pouring himself a third when there was an interruption. The door opened and through the chink in the curtains I saw Alice enter the room.

"What happened?" she demanded, and her soft country voice was indefinably harder and more resolute. "What did he say?"

Vere sat down in the chair again, seeming to crumple into the cushions. In a sudden flash of insight I saw then as clearly as I saw them both before me that Alice was the stronger of the two.

"It was no good." Vere was drinking again as she sat on the arm of his chair and put an arm around his shoulders. "He'll pay the debts but he won't advance me any more than the bare necessities. I'm reduced to the role of bailiff, it seems."

Alice's face was very set. "Tell me exactly what was said."

He told her, omitting nothing. When he had finished he half-rose with a glance at the decanter on the sideboard but she took the glass from him and poured the wine herself. I noticed that while he had his back to her she diluted the wine with water from the jug on the sideboard.

"Well, at least," she said as she brought the glass back to him, "we still have a roof over our heads."

"Temporarily." The wine was making him morose and apathetic. He seemed a mere pale shadow as he sat huddled in the vast armchair.

"It was a pity," said Alice, "that you had to go losing your temper and accusing him of murder."

"I didn't! All I said was—"

"He took it as an accusation, didn't he?"

"Well . . ."

"You really should be careful, dear," said Alice. "You really should. Let sleeping dogs lie. They decided Rodric killed your father, so leave it at that. Resurrecting old grudges and angers can only be dangerous to us, and if you offend George again—"

"He was having an affair with Mama, I swear it. I know when she looks at a man as she looked at him last year . . . Supposing Papa found out, threatened—"

"You really should let it be, dear. Just because your mother may have wished to have George as a lover, you've no proof that he did as she wanted, and you've no proof that he killed your father, nor will you ever have. Let it be, dearest! If you start resurrecting the past, who knows what might happen? Supposing someone found out that you came back earlier to Haraldsdyke that afternoon than you said you did? You told me you went straight to our room and lay down for a while as you weren't well, but I never saw you, did I, dear, and no one else saw you either. Supposing someone saw you slip into the house before your father was killed that afternoon and supposing they spoke up and said so if you went accusing George of murder—"

"Who could have seen me?" He was nervous; the wine spilled from his glass and stained the carpet. "No one saw me!"

"Mary might have done."

"She would have said so before now."

"Perhaps."

"Besides," he laughed uneasily "I had no reason for killing Papa."

"No, dear? People might think you did, though. He knew it was you, you know, and not Rodric who was involved with the Frenchies in the smuggling."

The glass jerked right out of Vere's hand and smashed to a hundred pieces. Vere's face went from a dull white to the color of ashes.

"He never knew that!"

"Rodric told him. Your father discovered the contraband hidden in the Thirty-Acre barn—"

"I know that, but he suspected Rodric! He never suspected me! He thought it was another of Rodric's escapades—he never suspected that his meanness over money had driven me to smuggling to help raise money for my plans."

"Yes, dear," said Alice, "he suspected Rodric, but Rodric denied it, why else do you suppose they had such a violent quarrel? In the end your father half-believed him, but not entirely. He shouted out: 'Neither of you will inherit anything under my new will! I'm finished with both of you!' he shouts. 'To hell with you,' said Rodric, shouting back, 'alter your will as you like—I no longer care!' But of course he didn't know that your father had already altered the will and made a new one the day before, leaving everything to George. I suppose he'd had his suspicions ever since he discovered the contraband two days earlier in the barn."

"But my God!" cried Vere, his voice trembling. "Why didn't you tell me before that you knew this?"

"I didn't want to worry you, dear. I saw no point in worrying you. And the less it was talked of the better. I didn't want anyone getting ideas and suspecting you of Lord knows what terrible things when it's quite plain Rodric was guilty."

"You really believe he was guilty?"

"He must have been, dear. He had the cause and he was there with your father in the library and both of them in towering rages."

"I suppose so. Lord knows I had no love for Rodric, but I hardly thought he'd be fool enough to kill the source of all his income."

"He didn't know your father had already altered his will to leave everything to George. He thought he would inherit money."

"True . . . But supposing George knew the will had

been changed in his favor? He was the only one of us who really benefited from Papa's death."

"You benefited too, dear. If he had lived he would have told the Watch at Rye that you were in league with the Frenchies."

"But my God—"

"Let it be, dear. Do as I say and let it be. Whatever happened in the past doesn't alter the present situation— it doesn't change the fact that we live here on George's charity only and if we offend George we'll find ourselves with no roof over our heads."

"Oh Alice, Alice . . ." He turned to her in despair and I saw her broad arms gathering him to her as if he were a little child and stroke his hair as he buried his face against her breast.

"There, there, dear," she said, much as she had spoken to her own children in the nursery that day. "There, there, my love . . ."

"I feel so helpless, so inadequate."

"Hush, don't say such things . . ."

They were silent, he clinging to her, she still clasping him in the comfort of her embrace, but presently he lifted his face to hers and kissed her on the lips. The atmosphere changed; there was passion in their embrace now, and such fervor in their gestures as I had never seen before between husband and wife. I glanced away, feeling that I was trespassing, and at the same time I was conscious of desolation as I saw the emptiness of my own marriage in a sickening moment of revelation. I was just wishing with all my heart that I could escape when Vere said suddenly: "I can't bear the insecurity of my position! What's to happen to our children? Even if we stay here, you nothing but an unpaid housekeeper and I nothing but a mere bailiff, there's no future for the children. George's children will inherit Haraldsdyke."

"If George has children," said Alice. "If he doesn't, our children will inherit."

"Why shouldn't George have children? He's fit and vigorous and the girl is young and healthy. She may already be pregnant, for all we know."

"I think not," said Alice. "Not at present."

"She will be before long." He buried his face in his hands again. "I don't know what to do," he said, his voice muffled, and then he raised his head in anger. "Why did George have to take up his inheritance? He had money in Vienna—and property too! What interest has he ever shown in Haraldsdyke? If he hadn't troubled to fulfill the conditions of the will by marrying an English girl within the year, the estate would have passed straight to Stephen, and I would have been trustee in my son's name till he came of age."

"It's no use saying that now, dear, not now that George has successfully claimed his inheritance and fulfilled the conditions of the will."

"And if the girl gets pregnant, it's the end of all our hopes! The devil take George Brandson! I wish—"

"Don't despair so, dear! You despair so easily. Why, a multitude of things may happen yet. Even if she does get pregnant, the child may be sickly and die. Or she may have a miscarriage. Or she may be barren. Or she may herself die."

A chill seemed to strike through that warm room. My blood seemed to run to ice and my mouth was dry.

"You're always so calm," Vere was saying, and to me at that moment it seemed as if he were speaking from a long way away, "so sensible . . . I don't know what I would ever do without you, Alice. Truthfully, I don't know what I would ever do if I didn't have you beside me at times such as these . . ."

They kissed. There was silence for a while. I glanced out of the window and saw my reflection in the glass pane, my eyes wide and dark in my white face.

"Come upstairs, my love," said Alice. "Come to bed. Don't sit here any more."

He rose obediently. The light caught his face and made him look haggard and drawn, and then he turned aside into the shadows and I could only see the gleam of his bright hair as he walked with Alice to the door.

They were gone; I was alone at last.

I was so stiff with tension, so unnerved by all I had overheard that I had to sit down and drink some of the wine from the decanter. Even after that I had difficulty in controlling my trembling limbs. However, finally I felt sufficiently recovered to return upstairs, and moving cautiously I stole outside and across the hall to the staircase.

The corridor above was in darkness and I stumbled unsteadily towards our rooms. When I reached the door of our sitting room at last I was so relieved I nearly fell across the threshold, but as I opened the door, I froze immediately in my tracks. For Esther was with Axel before the fireplace and it was obvious even to me in my confused state that she was very angry.

". . . chit of a girl," Esther was saying as I opened the door and halted abruptly on the threshold.

They both swung around to face me.

We all looked at one another in silence. Then:

"So there you are, my dear," said Axel, moving to-

wards me. "I was wondering what had happened to you."
And he drew me across the threshold and kissed me
lightly on the forehead.

Over his shoulder I saw Esther bite her lip. "I must
go," she said sharply. "Pray excuse me. Goodnight to you
both."

"Goodnight, Esther," Axel said courteously and held
the door open for her.

I said goodnight faintly as she swept past us out into
the corridor without another word.

Axel closed the door again and we were alone together.

"Are you all right?" he said at once, and no doubt he
was wondering why I had chosen to go wandering about
the house in a robe with my hair trailing loose upon my
shoulders. "You look a little pale."

"I—couldn't sleep." I went past him into the bedroom.
"In the end I went downstairs for a glass of wine in the
hope that it would make me sleepy."

"Did you find the wine?"

"There was a decanter in the dining room."

"Ah yes, of course, so there is. There's also a decanter
kept in the saloon in case you should ever need it. The
saloon is nearer than the dining room." He followed me
into the bedroom. "I'm glad you arrived back when you
did. I was having a rather difficult time with Esther."

I could not look at him for fear I might betray my
knowledge of his past relationship with her. Taking off
my robe and laying it aside, I slipped into bed once more
and closed my eyes.

"What did she want?" I managed to say.

"She seemed to have some idea that she was no longer
wanted here and would prefer to take a house in Rye.
Naturally I had to assure her that she was mistaken."

I knew instinctively that he was lying. I thought I knew all too well why Esther had chosen to come to his apartments to talk to him and why she had left immediately I had arrived on the scene. If she was angry, it was not because she felt she was now unwanted at Haraldsdyke; she was angry because she felt she was now unwanted in his bedroom. Only a fool would have chosen such a time to fan the flames of an old love affair, and certainly whatever else he might be, Axel was no fool.

"I think she's bored with country life," he was saying. "Vere has entertained very little during the past year, and Esther lived for her dinner parties and social occasions. To be honest, I think she wishes to take a house in Rye less because she feels unwanted here than because she is anxious to escape from this way of life now that she's free to do so."

"Why should she feel unwanted here?" I watched him through my lashes. He was undressing slowly, examining the fine linen of his shirt for any soiled marks.

"She was the mistress here for more than twenty-five years. Some women under such circumstances are reluctant to give way to a younger woman."

It was a clever excuse. It explained Esther's anger and her withdrawal as soon as I appeared.

"But why did she come to our apartments? She knew I had retired to bed."

"I had found you weren't in bed and as I went to the landing to look for you she came out of the drawing room and I asked her where you were. She said she had something to discuss with me in private and I suggested she come here." He took off his shirt and went into his adjoining dressing room.

I lay very still, my eyes half-closed, my limbs slowly

becoming tense and aching again. I was appalled how smoothly he could invent plausible lies.

At length he came out of the dressing room, snuffed the candles and slid into bed beside me. His limbs brushed mine.

"How cold you are," he said, drawing me closer to the warmth of his body. "I hope you haven't caught a chill."

"No . . ." I longed to press myself even closer to him and feel secure, but I was only conscious of nervousness and panic. "Axel—"

"Yes," he said. "Your state of health is delicate just now. I remember."

He did not sound altogether pleased. I sensed rather than felt his withdrawal from me.

"I—I'm sorry," I was stammering, feeling a mere ineffectual child cowed by a maze of subtle nightmares which surrounded me on all sides. "I'm so sorry, Axel—"

"Why should you be sorry?" he said. "You've done nothing wrong. Goodnight, my dear, and I hope you sleep well."

"Thank you," I whispered wretchedly. "Goodnight."

But sleep was impossible. I lay in that great bed, my limbs chilled and my feet feeling as ice, but my mind was not as numbed as my body and the longer I lay quietly in the darkness the more vivid my thoughts became. I began to toss and turn and when I finally crept closer to Axel for warmth, he turned abruptly, startling me for I thought he had been asleep.

"What's the matter?"

"Nothing. I'm a little cold."

"Cold! You're frozen! Come here."

I felt better lying in his arms. I even managed to drift off to sleep but awoke soon in panic after Vere, Alice and

Esther had all turned to me in a dream and said: "You'll really have to die, you know."

"My dear child," said Axel astonished as I sat up gasping in fright. "What on earth's possessed you tonight?" And he fired a match, lit the candle and drew me to him in consternation.

Such was my state of nerves that I could endure my silence no longer.

"I—I overheard a conversation between Vere and Alice when I was downstairs," I whispered desperately. "They don't want me to become pregnant—they want you to die childless so that their children can inherit—they want me to die . . ."

"Wait, wait, wait! I've never heard such a confused tale! My dear, Vere and Alice may, understandably, wish their children to inherit Haraldsdyke, but I can assure you that your death wouldn't help them at all, since there's no guarantee I wouldn't marry again—and again, if need be, though God forbid it . . . if they feel murderously inclined, which I doubt, then I'm the one they should dispose of, since I'm the only one who stands in their way at present."

He sounded so sane and balanced that I felt ashamed of my ridiculous panic.

"But they don't want me to have children, Axel—"

"No," he said, "I don't suppose they do. Neither would I, if I were in their situation. However, if you become pregnant there's nothing whatsoever they could do about it apart from cursing their misfortune anew."

"But—"

"Yes? What's troubling you now?"

"Perhaps—would it be possible . . . I mean, is it necessary that I have children now? Can I not wait a little and have them later?"

There was a silence. I saw the tolerant amusement die from his face and the old opaque expression descend like a veil over his eyes. At length he said dryly: "And how would you propose to arrange that, may I ask?"

"I—" My face was hot with embarrassment. "Surely—there are ways—"

"For whores," he said. "Not for ladies in your position."

I was without words. I could only lie there in a paralysis of shame and wish I had never spoken.

"You're not seriously alarmed by these chance remarks you overheard, are you?"

I shook my head in misery.

"Then why are you unanxious for children at present? I would of course see that you had the best medical care and attention throughout your confinement."

Speech was impossible. I could only stare at the sheet.

"I am most anxious for children," he said, "and not merely in order to establish myself at Haraldsdyke."

Hot tears scalded my eyes. It needed all my will-power and concentration to hold them in check. At last I managed to say in a very cold formal voice: "Please forgive me. I suddenly felt inadequate and too young for such a thing, but now I see I was being childish and stupid. I wish I hadn't mentioned it to you."

"Far from being inadequate and too young, I would say just the opposite. You will soon be eighteen, you're intelligent, capable and surprisingly mature in many ways. I'm sure you would be an excellent mother, and besides I think motherhood would probably be the best thing for you. You must have felt very alone in the world these last few weeks, and a child would alleviate your loneliness to some degree."

I was silent.

He kissed me lightly. "So no more talk about inadequacies and youth."

I did not reply.

He snuffed the candle so that we were in darkness once more and attempted to take me in his arms again, but presently I turned away from him and he made no attempt to stop me. My last conscious thought before I fell asleep was that if I asked Dame Joan the witch for a potion she would be sure to tell her daughter later, and then Alice and Vere would know with certainty that there was no threat to their children's inheritance for a while.

And once they knew that, I should be safe.

Five

I HAD PLANNED to steal away into the village some time
during the next day, but this proved to be impossible. I
had forgotten that Axel had invited the Shermans to dinner, and my morning was in fact spent with Alice preparing the menu, talking to the cook and supervising the
dusting of the furniture and the cleaning of the silver. The
strain of conducting the tasks was considerable even
though Alice was at my elbow to advise and instruct me;
I retired to my room soon after noon feeling exhausted
and glad to be alone for a while before it was time to
dress for dinner.

The guests were punctual; I was introduced to Mr.
James Sherman, the Brandsons' lawyer, who was a portly
gentleman in his forties, to his wife, Mrs. James, and to
their two daughters, Evelina and Annabella, both of
whom looked at me with frank jealousy, presumably be-

cause I had married the master of Haraldsdyke and they
had not. On meeting them I was not surprised that Axel
had looked elsewhere, and I turned with relief to greet
Mr. Charles Sherman, Mr. James' younger brother, who
was about the same age as Axel himself. Vere and Alice
soon appeared upon the scene, Vere making an effort to
appear relaxed and at ease, Alice seeming quietly self-
effacing. Mary sat in a corner and fidgeted, unnoticed. Ned
slunk in silently in the hope that no one would see him
and presently vanished as unobtrusively as he had arrived. It was left to Esther to make the grand entrance,
and she did so superbly, gliding into the room in a swirl
of black lace and diamonds, and moving forward to greet
each of the guests effusively.

All the men rose, young Mr. Charles Sherman preening
himself like a peacock and dancing across at once to
escort her to a couch where he could seat himself by her
side.

"Dear Esther," said Mrs. James sweetly, each word
barbed as a razor, "how well you look, even though the
tragedy was less than a year ago. Mourning does so become you."

"Dark colors have always suited me," said Esther with
a brilliant smile. "Besides only a young woman can look
well in pastel shades, don't you think?"

Mrs. James' gown was pale yellow.

"Pray tell us, Mrs. Brandson," said Miss Annabella
from beside me, "had you known your husband long before your marriage?"

I tried to concentrate on the conventional exchanges of
formal conversation.

With a remorseless inevitability, the evening crept
along its tedious path. In comparison with the small din-

ner parties which my mother had been accustomed to give from time to time, I found the visitors boring, their outlook provincial and their conversation devoid of any subject which might have interested me. The prospect of the remainder of my life being filled with such gestures in the name of hospitality and entertainment depressed me beyond words.

At long last when they were gone and their carriage was rattling off down the drive to the Marsh road below, I retreated to my room as rapidly as possible, kicked off my dainty high-heeled satin slippers and shouted irritably for Marie-Claire to set me free from the agonies of my tight laced corset. I had already dismissed her and was moodily brushing my hair when Axel came into the room.

I tried to smile. "I hope the evening passed satisfactorily to you, Axel."

"Yes indeed," he said with a spontaneity I had not expected. "You were splendid and the Shermans were very impressed with you. I was exceedingly pleased."

"I'm—very glad." And indeed I was relieved that my boredom had not been apparent. But later when he emerged from his dressing room he said casually: "No doubt it must have been very dull for you after the sparkling dinner parties of London."

I felt myself blush. "Different, certainly," I said, "but not altogether dull."

"It was dull for me," he said, "but then I'm accustomed to Vienna and even London would be dull to me in comparison." He paused to look at me, he standing by the bed, I leaning back upon the pillows, and as our glances met it seemed for one brief instant that a flash of understanding passed between us, a moment of being "en rapport" with one another.

He smiled. I smiled too, hesitantly. For a second I thought he was going to make some complimentary or even affectionate remark, but all he said in the end was simply: "You would like Vienna. I think I shall have to take you there one day."

Perhaps it was the relief of escaping at last from the tedium of the evening or perhaps it was because of that strange moment when we had exchanged glances and smiled, but for the first time I longed for him, for a release from loneliness, for a glimpse of what marriage might have been. The dinner party, as so often happens when the familiar is placed side by side with the horror of nightmare, had made my frightened thoughts recede into dim shadows from which I had no wish for them to emerge, and in the effort to seek a final oblivion for my unhappiness I turned to him absolutely and sought his embraces with a passion which must have taken him unawares. Passion sparked passion; flame ignited flame. I knew instinctively, as one knows such things, that after his initial astonishment he was concious of nothing save the burning of our emotions and the whirling painful spiral of desire.

The night passed; sleep when it came was deep and untroubled, and then towards dawn the fears and doubts and anxieties in my mind began to clamor for recognition after the long hours of being forcibly suppressed. I awoke at seven in the agonized grip of a nightmare and lay trembling between the sheets for some time. And as I lay waiting for the day to break, the mist rolled in across the Marsh from the sea and thickened in icy shrouds around the walls of Haraldsdyke.

It was Sunday. I learned that the Brandsons customari-
ly attended matins at Haraldsford Church every week,
and accordingly after Axel and I had breakfasted together
in our rooms I dressed formally in my dark blue woolen
traveling habit in preparation for braving the chill of the
mist later on.

The weather was not inviting. From our windows it
was barely possible to see to the end of the short drive,
and beyond the walls surrounding the grounds the dank
whiteness blotted out all trace of the view south over the
Marsh to Rye and the sea.

"A true November day," said Axel wryly as he sat
down to breakfast with a glance at the scene beyond the
window pane.

I felt ill-at-ease with him that morning for reasons I
did not fully understand; the nightmare had wakened me
with all my fears revived and my sense of being in any
way in accord with Axel had vanished, just as my memory of the normality of the dinner party had receded. I now
felt curiously ashamed of my demonstrative emotions of
the previous night, and my shame manifested itself in an
instinctive withdrawal from him. He rose more cheerful
and good-humored than I had ever seen him before, but I
made no effort at conversation and while not ignoring his
attentiveness, I found myself unable to respond to it.

Presently he sensed my mood and fell silent.

"Are you feeling well?" he said at last. "I had forgotten
your health had been delicate recently."

"Thank you," I said, "but I'm quite recovered."

He said nothing further but I sensed him watching me
carefully and at last, almost in irritation, I raised my
glance to meet his. He smiled but I looked away and
when I looked at him again the animation was gone from

his face and his eyes were opaque and without expression once more.

When he had finished his breakfast he went downstairs, for he was already dressed, and I summoned Marie-Claire. Some time later I followed him downstairs, my muff, bonnet and redingote in my hands so that I would not be obliged to return to my rooms before going to church, and wandered into the saloon to see what time it was according to the grandfather clock there.

The fire was alight in the grate but the room was still damp and cold. At first I thought it was also empty and then I saw Mary huddled in one of the tall armchairs near the hearth. Her hands were outstretched towards the flames and I could see the chilblains on her fingers as I drew closer. She smiled nervously at me, and muttered some half-intelligible greeting.

"It's a most unpleasant morning, is it not?" I said abruptly, sitting down opposite her. "Where is everyone? Isn't it time to leave for church yet?"

"I suppose we're the first to be ready," she said, stating the obvious. "Perhaps we're a trifle early."

We sat in silence for a while, both feeling awkward in each other's presence. In the distance I could hear Alice talking and Vere's indistinct response and then Axel called from somewhere close at hand: "Did you order the carriage to the door, Vere?"

"I sent Ned to the stables with the message."

There was more conversation. I heard Esther's voice then and Axel saying "Good morning" to her. Footsteps echoed in the hall.

"Everyone seems to be assembling now," I murmured to Mary, and then saw to my astonishment that there were tears in her eyes. As she saw that I had noticed them she blushed and made an awkward gesture with her hands.

"Sunday mornings always remind me of Rodric," she said shame-faced. "I so much used to enjoy traveling with him to church. He is not—was not—very reverent towards the rector but he used to make me laugh no matter how much I disapproved of his jokes on principle."

I stared at her curiously. It was not the first time, I suddenly realized, that she had referred to Rodric in the present tense. To do so once was a natural enough mistake; twice was still excusable, but I was sure she had made the error on more than two occasions. Wondering whether it was simply an affectation assumed to underline her grief or whether it had any other possible significance, I said off-handedly: "Why do you so often talk about Rodric as if he's not dead at all? You're constantly forgetting to talk of him in the past tense! Is it because you think he may be still alive?"

She stared at me round-eyed. Her mouth was open in surprise and I could see that one of her teeth was discolored with decay. And then as I watched her in mounting fascination she turned bright red, licked her lips and glanced wildly around the room to see if anyone had slipped in to eavesdrop while her back had been turned. I glanced around too, but of course there was no one there. The door was slightly open, just as I had left it, and from the hall came the vague sounds of footsteps and snatches of conversation.

"—my best fur," Esther was saying far away. "Quite ravaged by moth . . . Vere, you're not taking the child to church, are you?"

"Stephen behaves very well in church," said Alice,

"and I shall take him to see my mother afterwards. Let me take him, Vere. Here, precious, come to Mama . . ."

"Where's your wife, George?"

"And Mary!" said Esther, faintly exasperated. "Where's Mary? That child is always late . . ."

"Mary?" I said in a low voice.

But she was shifting uneasily in her chair. "He's dead," she mumbled. I had never heard a lie told so badly. "Dead." She stood up, fumbling with her gloves, not looking at me.

"I don't believe you," I said, curiosity making my voice sharp and hard. "You're lying. Tell me the truth."

The poor girl was so nervous of me that she dropped both her gloves on the floor and started to grovel for them helplessly, but I was ruthless. "So he's alive," I said, pitting my will against hers and watching her defenses crumble beneath the pressure. "How do you know? Answer me! How do you know he didn't drown in the Marsh that day?"

My voice had risen in my determination to extract the truth. I saw her put her finger to her lips in an agony of worry lest someone should hear us.

"Shhh . . . oh please—"

"How do you know he didn't—"

"I saw him." She was half-whispering, still motioning me to speak more softly. "I saw him come back to the house after George had told us he had found Rodric's horse and hat by a bog in the Marsh."

I stared at her.

"I—I was so upset when I heard the news of his death," she said, "that I went to see Ned first, but Ned was too upset himself to comfort me. Then I went to Rodric's room to sit for a while with his possessions around me, I couldn't believe he was dead . . ."

"And he came back."

"Yes, I heard footsteps and hid behind a curtain because I didn't want to be found there. I didn't want to talk to anyone. And then—and then . . . he came in. At first I thought it was a ghost—I—I nearly fainted . . . He came into the room, took some money out of a drawer, glanced at his watch and then went out again. He wasn't in the room for more than a few seconds."

"And you didn't speak to him? You didn't call out?"

"I was too stunned—I was nearly fainting with the shock."

"Quite. What did you do then?"

"I waited for him to come back."

"And didn't he?"

"No, that was what was so strange. I waited and waited and waited but he never came. I never saw him again."

"But didn't you tell anyone what you'd seen? Didn't you—"

"Only George."

"Axel!" I felt a sudden weakness in my knees. "Why Axel?"

"Well, I thought and thought about what I should do and then since George was the one who broke the news about Rodric's death I decided to tell him what had happened. But he didn't believe me. He said it was a—a hallucination born of shock and he advised me not to tell anyone or people would think my reason had been affected . . . So I said nothing more. But I have gone on hoping. Every day I go to wait in his room in case—"

"But you did see him," I said slowly, "didn't you. It wasn't your imagination. You really did see him."

My belief in her story gave her confidence. "Yes," she said. "Yes, I swear I did. I did see him. I know Rodric was alive after George told me he was dead."

There was a draft from the threshold as the door swung wider on its hinges. Esther's voice said harshly: "What nonsense! What a despicable tale to tell, Mary Moore! You should be ashamed of yourself!" As I whirled around with a start I saw she was trembling in every limb. "Rodric's dead," she said, and her voice too was trembling now. "I loved him, but he's dead and I accepted his death, but you—you stupid foolish child—have to invent fantastic stories of him being alive just to please your sense of the dramatic!" She was crying; tears welled in her eyes and she pressed her hands against her cheeks. "How *dare* you upset me like this—"

Vere was behind her suddenly, and Alice. Vere said: "Mama, what is it? What's the matter?" and beyond Alice I heard Axel's voice say sharply: "Esther?"

But Esther did not hear him. Fortified by Vere's arms around her she was weeping beautifully into a delicate lace handkerchief while poor Mary, also smitten with tears, howled that she hadn't meant what she said, Rodric was dead, she had never seen him return to his room late last Christmas Eve, she was merely indulging in wishful thinking. . . .

"Stop!" Axel exclaimed sternly in his most incisive voice, and there was an abrupt silence broken only by Mary's snuffles. "Mary, you should surely know by now that you must not try to impose your own dream world on other people. Haven't I warned you about that before? Day-dreaming is selfish at the best of times, a dangerous self-indulgence. . . . Come, Esther, the child didn't mean to upset you. Forgive her—it wasn't done maliciously. Now, are we all ready to leave? We shall be very late if we delay here much longer."

We were all ready. Within two minutes we were on our way to the church at Haraldsford, and throughout the service that followed I tried to make up my mind whether Mary had been telling the truth or not. In the end I came to the conclusion, as Axel had done, that her "vision" of Rodric must have been a hallucination born of shock. After all, I reasoned, if Rodric really had arranged a faked death for himself in the Marsh, why had he then risked discovery by returning to the house? And if he had indeed returned to the house, how had he managed to vanish into thin air after Mary had seen him? And finally if he were alive today, where was he? Despite my romantic inclination to believe him alive, my common sense would not wholly allow me to do so. He must be dead, I told myself. If he were alive, the situation would make no sense.

And yet for some hours to come I found myself wondering.

My mother had been a Roman Catholic once long ago before her flight from France and her struggles for existence in England, but her faith had ebbed with her fortunes and she had made no protest when a succession of nannies, governesses and finally schools had firmly imprinted Alexander and myself with the stamp of the Church of England. This was probably for the best; at that time there was still a large amount of prejudice against Catholics and besides, my father, although amoral and irreligious, was always quick to champion the Church of England against what he called "damned Papist non-sense."

The little church at Haraldsford was, of course, as are all Parish churches in this country, Protestant, the rector firmly adhering to the principles of the Church of England. As we entered the ancient porch that morning and stepped into the nave I saw a host of curious eyes feast upon us in welcome and realized that the villagers had flocked to church en masse for a glimpse of the new master of Haraldsdyke and his wife. Axel led the way to the Brandson pew without looking to right or to left but I glanced quickly over the gaping faces and wondered what they were thinking. It was, after all, less than a year since Robert Brandson and Rodric had come to this church. I sat down beside Axel, imagining more clearly than ever now the scandal that must have thrived at the time of their deaths, the gossip and speculation, the endless rumors whispering and reverberating through the community.

Throughout the service it seemed to me that I could almost feel the gaze of several dozen pairs of eyes boring remorselessly into my back, but of course that was a mere fantasy, and when I stole a glance over my shoulder during the prayers I saw that no one was watching me.

The sermon began. The child Stephen began to shift restlessly between his parents, and then Alice pulled him on to her lap and he was content for a while. I remembered that Alice was taking him to see her mother after the service was over, and I began to wonder how I could also manage to see Dame Joan that morning. Perhaps this afternoon I would be able to slip away from the house and walk back to the village. It was a mere mile, after all.

It wouldn't take long. But supposing someone saw me leave, asked questions when I came back . . . I should have to have an excuse for returning to the village on such a chill misty afternoon.

During the final prayers and blessing I managed to roll my muff surreptitiously under the pew. No one noticed.

After the service was over, we paused to exchange greetings with the rector and then returned to the carriage while Alice took the child down the road to her mother's house and Ned disappeared silently in the direction of the "Black Ram" for a tankard of ale. Within ten minutes we were back at Haraldsdyke. I managed to hide my bare hands in my wide sleeves so that no one should notice my muff was missing, and hastened to my rooms to change into a fresh gown.

Dinner was served earlier that day, I discovered, partly to revive everyone after the visit to church and partly to help the servants have a more restful evening than usual. With the exception of Alice, who had evidently decided to spend some time with her mother, we all sat down in the dining room soon after two o'clock.

Ned slunk in a moment later. I thought Axel was going to censure him but he took no notice and after Ned had muttered a word of apology nothing further was said to him. I noticed, not for the first time, how his mother always ignored him entirely. During the meal she conversed with Vere and managed to draw Axel into the conversation while also taking pains to address a remark to me now and again. I was careful to smile and reply sweetly, suppressing any trace of the dislike I felt for her, but by the end of the meal I was wondering if there really was any chance of her taking a house in Rye. Perhaps now that she was at last free and her year of mourning was nearly over, she would find herself a suitable husband and remarry.

I watched her, remembering what Ned had told me, remembering that she had been estranged from her husband for the twenty years before his death even though they had continued to live under the same roof. She must have hated him. What a relief it must have been for her, I thought, to have found herself a widow . . .

Alice came back just as we were finishing dinner, and said she would eat in the nursery with Stephen and the other children. Presently, Esther, Mary and I withdrew to the drawing room and within ten minutes I excused myself from them on the pretense that I wanted to rest for an hour or so. Once I was safely in my apartments I changed from the gown I had worn for dinner, donned my thick traveling habit once more and tip-toed out of the house by the back stairs.

No one saw me.

Outside the fog was thickening and I was soon out of sight of the house. It was unnaturally quiet, the fog muffling all sound, and soon the stillness, the gathering gloom and the eerie loneliness of the Marsh road began to prey upon my imagination. I continually thought I heard footsteps behind me, but when I stopped to listen there was nothing, just the thick heavy silence, and I came to the conclusion that the noise of my footsteps must in some strange way be re-echoing against the wall of mist to create an illusion of sound.

I was never more relieved when after several minutes of very brisk walking I saw the first cottages on the outskirts of the village and then the tower of Haraldsford church looming mysteriously out of the mist like some

THE SHROUDED WALLS 157

ghostly castle in a fairytale. I hurried past it. The village street was empty and deserted, chinks of light showing through the shuttered windows of the cottages, a lamp burning by the doorway of the "Black Ram." Everyone seemed to be indoors to escape the weather. Two minutes later I was by the door of Dame Joan's cottage on the other side of the village and tapping nervously on the ancient weatherbeaten wood.

There was no answer. I tapped again, the unreasoning panic rising within me, and then suddenly the door was opening and she was before me, broad and massive-boned, her curious eyes interested but not in the least astonished; behind her I could see a black cat washing his paws before a smoldering peat fire.

"Come in, Mrs. George." She sounded strangely businesslike, as if there was nothing strange about the mistress of Haraldsdyke paying a social call on her at four o'clock on a dark November afternoon. It occurred to me in a moment of macabre fantasy that she seemed almost to have been expecting me, and then I put the thought aside as ridiculous.

"Thank you," I said, crossing the threshold. "I hope I'm not disturbing you."

"No indeed." She drew a wooden chair close to the fire for me and pushed the cat out of the way. I half-expected the cat to hiss and spit at this casual dismissal from the fireside but far from being incensed it rubbed itself against her skirts and purred lovingly. When she sat down opposite me a moment later it jumped up into her lap and she began to stroke it with her broad flat fingers.

"Some herb tea, Mrs. George? Warm you after your walk."

"No—no, thank you very much."

She smiled. I suddenly noticed that the pupils of her strange eyes were no more than black dots. They were very odd eyes indeed.

I felt unnerved suddenly, overcome by a gust of fright, and wished I had not come. I was just wondering how I could retreat without it seeming as if I were running away when she said: "Alice was here a little while past with my grandson. A beautiful child."

"Yes," I said. "Yes, indeed."

"You'll be having children of your own soon, I've no doubt."

"I—" Words stuck in my throat.

She nodded secretly and waited.

My hands clutched the material of my habit in a hot moist grip. "I was very ill this summer," I invented, and somehow I had the unpleasant suspicion that she would know I was lying. "My health is still delicate, and the doctors all said I should be careful. I am anxious to avoid pregnancy for a little while yet."

She nodded again. The firelight glinted in her eyes and gave them a strange reddish cast. Her lips were curved in a smile still and her teeth seemed sharp and predatory. I was by now quite speechless. For a moment there was a silence broken only by the purring of the cat in her lap. Then:

"There's an herb," said the witch. "Very helpful, it is, if taken properly. I've made many a potion with pennyroyal."

"A potion?"

"I have a jar now ready for Mary Oaks out at Tansedge Farm. Fourteen children in sixteen years and couldn't take no more. I've been making the potion for her for three years now."

"And she hasn't—during that time—"

"Not even the ghost of a child, Mrs. George. For three years."

"I—see . . ."

"Let me give you the jar I have ready for Mary Oaks and then I can make another potion for her tomorrow."

"If—if that's possible . . . I—have a sovereign here . . ."

"Lord love you, Mrs. George, what would I be doing with gold sovereigns? Alice sees I don't want for anything, and besides I never go to Rye to spend coin. Bring me a gift some time, if you like, but no sovereigns."

So in the end it was all extraordinarily easy. After she had given me the potion I forced myself to stay a few minutes longer for politeness' sake, and then I escaped as courteously as possible. As I stepped outside the relief seemed to strike me with an almost physical intensity. My legs were shaking and the palms of my hands were still moist with sweat.

The guilt began to assail me as soon as I walked away from the cottage through the village to the church. I began to feel ashamed of myself, horror-stricken at what I had done. I had reduced myself to the level of a loose woman, sought medication which was undoubtedly sinful and wicked in the eyes of the church. If Axel were ever to find out . . .

When I reached the church I was trembling in a wave of nervous reaction and remorse. I eased open the heavy oak door and slipped into the dark nave, my eyes blurred with tears, and stumbled to the Brandson pew where I retrieved my muff and sat down for a moment to think. I prayed for forgiveness for my wickedness and in a wave of emotional fervor which was entirely foreign to my usual passive acceptance of religion, I begged God to un-

derstand why I had acted so shamefully and promised to
have children later in life when I was not so frightened or
uncertain of myself and my husband.

At last, my guilt assuaged to a degree where I could
dry my eyes and pull myself together, I stood up, walked
briskly down the nave and wrenched open the heavy door
with a quick tug of the wrist.

The shock I received then was like a dagger thrust beneath my ribs.

For there, waiting for me in the shelter of the porch,
was none other than my husband, Axel Brandson.

My muff concealed the jar containing Dame Joan's potion but I could feel the hot color rushing to my face to
proclaim my guilty conscience. I gave a loud exclamation
and then hastily exaggerated my reaction of surprise to
conceal any trace of guilt.

"How you startled me!" I gasped, leaning faintly
against the doorpost. "Did you follow me here?"

His face was very still; he was watching me closely. "I
saw you go into the church. I had come from the house to
look for you."

"Oh . . . But how did you know I'd left the house?"

"Esther said you'd gone to your room, but when I went
to look for you I only found your maid looking mystified
since you appeared to have changed into your outdoor
habit again."

"My muff was missing," I said. "I realized I must have
left it in church this morning."

"Why didn't you send one of the servants to collect it?
To venture beyond the walls of Haraldsdyke on an after-

noon such as this was very foolish, not merely from the point of view of exposing yourself to such a chill, unhealthy mist, but also on account of the risk of meeting a stray peddler on the road."

"I—didn't think of it."

"I was extremely worried."

"I'm sorry," I said subdued. "I'm very sorry, Axel."

"Well, we'll say no more about it but I trust you'll be more sensible in future."

He made me feel like a child of six. However, so relieved was I that he had not seen me leave Dame Joan's cottage that I was quite prepared to tolerate any reproof without complaint. Accordingly I stood before him meekly with downcast eyes and said that yes, I would be more sensible in the future, and presently we left the church and set off back through the heavy mist to Haraldsdyke.

He scarcely spoke half a dozen words to me on the way home, and I knew he was still angry. I also had an unpleasant intuition that he was suspicious, although he gave no indication that he had disbelieved my story. We walked along the road as quickly as I could manage, and even while we walked the darkness was blurring the mist before us and making the gloom twice as obscure. By the time we reached the walls of Haraldsdyke it was scarcely possible to see anything which was not within a few feet of our eyes. The front door was unlocked. Axel opened it and we stepped into the hall.

The house was curiously still. I was just about to remark on the unnatural silence which prevailed everywhere when there was the slam of a door from upstairs and the next moment Vere appeared on the landing and came swiftly down the stairs towards us. He was wearing his riding habit and his face was a shade more pale than usual.

"Mary has just been taken ill," he said. "I'm riding to Winchelsea for Dr. Salter."

Alice was very distressed. "I left the nursery where I had had dinner with the children," she said to me, "and went to the drawing room. You'd just left to go to your room. Mary was huddled around the fireplace and it was damp in the room despite the fire so I suggested we had some tea to warm us all. I went down to the kitchens to give the order myself—I always like to spare the servants as much as possible on Sundays. Presently George and Vere came up from the dining room where they had been sitting with their port, and Vere had the tray of tea with him—he'd met the maid in the hall and said he would take the tray up for her. George lingered for a while, handing around the tea as I poured it out, but after a few minutes he said he was going to look for you; however, everyone else, except Ned who had disappeared somewhere as usual, stayed and drank tea for a while."

We were outside the door of Mary's room in the dark passage, I still wearing my traveling habit, Alice carrying a flickering candle, her hand on the latch of the door. Axel had gone out to the stables with Vere in an effort to dissuade him from attempting the ride to Winchelsea in the thick mist.

"And when did Mary become ill?" I said uneasily.

"Perhaps half an hour later. The maid had collected the tea-tray and taken it downstairs, and as the maid went out Mary suddenly said she felt very sick and was going to vomit."

"And—"

"And she did, poor girl. All over the new rug. Esther—Vere's mother—was most upset. About the rug, I mean. Then she saw Mary was really ill and became alarmed. We got Mary to bed and she was still ill and complaining of pains so Vere said he would ride at once to Winchelsea for Dr. Salter."

"The mist is very thick," I said uncertainly. "And now that night has come it's almost impossible to see anything."

"I know—I wish he wouldn't go, but I suppose he must. The poor girl's so ill."

"Do you think it's anything infectious?" I had had a morbid dread of illness since a childhood friend had died of cholera.

"No, she often suffers from her stomach. No doubt she's eaten something disagreeable to her."

I shivered a little. I could remember stories of people dying in twenty-four hours after being struck down with a violent sickness and a pain in the right side.

"You're cold," said Alice, mistaking the cause of my shivering. "You shouldn't be lingering here. Hurry to your room and change into something warm before you catch a chill."

I took her advice and knelt on the hearth of the sitting room for several minutes while I stretched out my hands towards the fire. Some time later when I had changed my clothes and had returned to sit by the fireside, Axel came into the room.

"Vere insisted on going to Winchelsea," he said abruptly. "I wish he hadn't but I suppose it was the right thing to do. He should be all right if he keeps to the road, and the Marsh road at least is hard to wander from since it's raised above the level of the surrounding land. It's not as if he intended to cut across the Marsh as Rodric did."

There was a shadow in my mind suddenly, a strange shaft of uneasiness. Perhaps it was the recollection of how Rodric had died, or perhaps it was merely the mention of his name. It was as if Rodric was the center of an invisible whirlpool of dissonance, the unseen cause of all the trouble existing beneath the roof of Haraldsdyke. It was as if everything began and ended with Rodric. I thought of him then, as I had so often thought of him during the past week, and suddenly it seemed that his vivid personality had never been more real to me and that I knew every nuance of his turbulent personality, each new facet of his charm.

"Mary was always so fond of Rodric," I said aloud, but speaking more to myself.

"Yes, she idolized him," said Axel absently. "It's quite a normal phase for a girl her age to go through, I believe."

And then suddenly I saw it all, saw Mary saying "I did see him—I know Rodric was alive after George told us he was dead," saw everyone listening to her in the doorway, saw Axel's impatient expression as he dismissed her memories as a past hallucination of no importance. "I swear I saw him," Mary had said, and no one, not even I, had believed her—no one except perhaps one person who had at once realized Mary was in possession of a dangerous truth . . .

I stood up.

Axel glanced at me in surprise. "What's the matter?"

"Nothing . . . I'm a little restless." I went over to the window. My mouth was quite dry.

Presently I said: "I wonder how Mary is." My voice sounded as if my throat were parched.

"Perhaps we should go and find out." He was already moving to the door as if glad of the chance to accomplish something positive.

I followed him, my heart bumping against my ribs.

Esther came out of Mary's room just as we were approaching it. She looked strangely uncomposed and worried.

"George," she said, ignoring me, "I think I'm going to give her some of my laudanum—Doctor Salter gave me a little, you know, to help me sleep after Robert's death. Do you think that's wise? Normally I would be reluctant to give laudanum to a child, but she's in pain and Alice suggested we should use it to relieve the suffering . . ."

"Let me see the laudanum." He went with her into the bedroom and to my great relief turned to me on the threshold and said: "You'd better go back to our rooms, my dear. I'll let you know if there's anything you can do."

I went mutely back to our sitting room, but found myself unable to sit down for any length of time. I kept thinking of everyone drinking tea in the drawing room. Everyone had been there except Ned. Vere had brought the tray of tea upstairs. And Axel had handed around the cups . . .

I began to pace restlessly about the room. I was being absurd, hysterical, over-imaginative. Mary had a weak digestion. Something had disagreed with her.

Alice made toadstool poison for the mice in the cellar. Perhaps it was kept in jars in the pantry. Perhaps anyone could go there and remove as much as was required. Perhaps . . .

I went out into the corridor but the house was quiet and still, silent as a tomb, so I went back into the room again.

If only my nerves were not already so overwrought, then perhaps melodramatic thoughts would be easier to avoid. As it was, my mind refused to be reasonable, even though I tried to tell myself that Vere would eventually arrive with the doctor, that the doctor would prescribe something to soothe the digestion, that tomorrow Mary would be weak but at least partially recovered.

The evening dragged on.

At length, unable to bear the suspense, I went to Mary's room but there was no news, except that she was still very ill. Esther was sitting with her. I did not venture into the room itself. When I knocked on the door Alice came out of the room into the passage to talk to me again in a low voice.

"George went downstairs to wait for Vere," she said. "Pray God the doctor arrives soon."

But it was another hour before the doctor arrived, and even when he finally came he was too late.

Mary died at one o'clock the following morning.

Six

FOR SEVERAL HOURS I was too appalled to do anything.
As if in a daze I heard the doctor cautiously diagnose the
sickness of which I had heard before, the illness manifested by vomiting and a pain in the right side. I heard Esther
talking of notifying Mary's distant relatives, of making
arrangements for the funeral. I heard Axel arranging for
the doctor to stay the night so that he did not have to
travel back to Winchelsea until the fog had cleared. I
heard the clocks chime and doors close and footsteps
come and go, and all I could think was that the nightmare
was closing in on all sides of me, that Mary had died after
she had revealed to everyone, not merely to Axel, how
she had seen Rodric alive after his presumed death in the
Marsh last Christmas Eve.

At three o'clock Axel ordered me to bed to snatch
some sleep before dawn, but sleep was impossible. Even

when Axel came to bed himself half an hour later and fell
into an uneasy sleep beside me I still found it impossible
to relax my limbs and drift into unconsciousness. At four
o'clock I rose from the bed, put on a thick woolen wrap
to ward off the cold and went next door into the sitting
room. It was pitch dark, but finally I managed to light a
candle and sat down, teeth chattering, at the secretaire to
write to Alexander.

"If you have not already left Harrow," I wrote, "please
leave now. I know not what to think of events taking
place here, and am very frightened indeed. Robert
Brandson's ward Mary Moore died tonight, and although
the doctor diagnosed death due to an inflammation of the
lower intestine, I have reason to believe she was poisoned. I think she knew something relating to the deaths
of both Robert and Rodric Brandson, something which
was apparently so important that she was killed before
she could repeat her story enough times to persuade people to take it seriously. If this is so, then Robert Brandson's murderer was not Rodric at all but someone else—
and this possibility is not as unlikely as it sounds. Any of
them could be guilty, except possibly Ned, the youngest
son, who isn't Robert Brandson's son anyway but the
result of Esther Brandson's infidelity years ago. All of
them had cause. Vere had been involved in smuggling
to raise money to pay his debts, and his father had found
out and was threatening to tell the Watch at Rye of
his activities—this would have been very grave, as apart
from the smuggling Vere was dealing with the Frenchman
Delancey, and this might constitute treason since we're at
war with France. It's generally thought that Rodric was
the one who was in league with Delancey in this manner,
but a conversation I overheard between Vere and Alice

proved that Vere was the guilty one and that Rodric wasn't involved.

"So Rodric really didn't have the motive for murder— unless it was that his father, believing him guilty, had threatened to cut him out of his will; in fact Robert Brandson had already done this in a new will in which he left all to Axel, but this wasn't generally known and I suppose Rodric might have killed his father in the hope of forestalling any change of will. But I don't think Rodric was the kind of man to have done this. To begin with I don't think he would have taken his father's threat seriously. It sounds to me as if Robert Brandson was a man who shouted and roared a great deal in rage but who seldom carried out his worst threats. I don't think Rodric would have believed there was any danger of him being disinherited.

"But if Vere knew that his father believed him guilty of treason and smuggling, that would have been very serious indeed; even if Robert Brandson didn't inform the Watch at Rye (as he threatened to do) he would certainly have eliminated Vere from his will. And that would have been very serious for a man with a wife and three children and neither land nor independent income of any kind.

"Esther Brandson too had cause for murder. She was estranged from her husband and had been for nearly twenty years, since before Ned was born. I'm almost certain she must have hated him and loathed the isolation and rural position of Haraldsdyke. At the time of his death she was having an affair with another man, and it's possible Robert Brandson found out about this or perhaps she thought she would have a new life with this new lover if only her husband were dead. I suppose it's less likely that a woman could have wielded the butt of the gun to club Robert Brandson to death, but Esther is tall and I suspect fairly strong. And if she were enraged she would have even twice her normal strength.

"Axel too had cause for killing his father. He was Esther's lover. He also benefited under his father's new will, a fact which might or might not have been known to him, but if he did know about it, he wouldn't have wanted that new will to be changed; and if his father found out about the affair with Esther the will would naturally have been altered to eliminate Axel as a beneficiary.

"They all had the opportunity. It was generally supposed that Vere was out on the estate till late in the day, but I heard Alice say that he came back to the house much earlier, although no one saw him. Esther apparently discovered the body, but Axel went with her downstairs to the hall, according to Ned who saw them leave Esther's rooms together, and a long time elapsed between their descent to the hall and Esther's screams which marked the discovery of her husband's body.

"But now listen to what happened to Mary. When Axel finally returned to Haraldsdyke later that day with the news that Rodric had apparently drowned in the Marsh Mary was so upset that she went to sit in his, Rodric's, room to meditate among his possessions, and it was here that *she saw* Rodric slip into the room for two seconds to get some money and then slip out again. And Rodric was supposed to be dead! She told Axel, who dismissed the story as a fantasy, and was too timid to go on reiterating the tale although she herself remained convinced she had not imagined the scene. On the day she died she revealed this story to me, and her revelations were ultimately overheard by Esther, Vere, Alice, and Axel, who again dismissed the story in such a way that ever I was convinced Mary had been the victim of her imagination. But then she died. I think she was poisoned. Alice keeps poison for the mice somewhere in the kitchens and anyone could have had access to it.

"If Mary really did see Rodric, and I now think she did, does this mean that Rodric is alive today? Whatever it means it seems clear that if she did see him, he didn't drown accidentally in the Marsh as everyone thinks he did. And obviously the murderer wants this story of his accidental death to stand unquestioned so that Rodric can so conveniently take the blame for his father's murder. For instance, if Rodric himself was murdered the authorities would surely look at Robert Brandson's death in a very different light. But if Rodric was murdered, where's his body? And if he's alive, why isn't he here to denounce the true murderer and protest his innocence? Truly I don't know what to think. I don't know for certain that Axel is a murderer, but what's worse, I don't know for certain that he's not. All I know with certainty is that there's a murderer under this roof and I want nothing except to escape.

"Please come. I don't think I've ever needed you more than I do now, and you're all I have."

After I had read the letter through twice I folded it, sealed it, and wrote "ALEXANDER FLEURY, HARROW SCHOOL, HARROW, MIDDLESEX" in large letters on the outside. Then, feeling strangely comforted by having confided my worst fears and most hideous thoughts to paper, I left the sealed letter on the blotter and returned to bed where I fell into an exhausted dreamless sleep almost at once.

I must have slept for a long time for when I awoke the mist was gone, the sun was streaming through the gap in the curtains and I was alone in bed.

I sat up. The clock on the mantelshelf indicated it was eleven o'clock, and as I stared in horrified disbelief at the lateness of the hour I heard the sound of voices in the adjoining room. I slid out of bed, drew on my heavy woolen wrap and crossed the floor to the door. Axel was talking to Esther. I heard first his level tones, and then the sound of her voice raised in anger, and I knew at once that something had happened to upset her considerably.

I opened the door and then froze in amazement, hardly able to believe my eyes at what I saw.

For Esther had in her hands my letter to Alexander, and someone, I saw to my fright and fury, someone had broken the seal.

Anger overcame all fear. Conscious of nothing except that an outrage had been committed I stormed into the room and, shaking with rage, snatched the letter from Esther's fingers before she could even draw breath to speak.

"How dare you!" The words choked in my throat. I could barely see. "How dare you open my letter!"

But she took barely five seconds to recover from the shock of my entrance. "And how dare *you!*" she flung back at me. "How dare you write such libelous filth about me in a letter to a schoolboy! I've never been so insulted in all my life!"

"Truth is a defense to libel!" I retorted, "And only a woman who behaved like a deceitful trollop running from lover to lover would stoop to the debasement of opening another's letters—"

"Wait," said Axel icily, and when Esther took no notice, he raised his voice until she fell silent. "Please—no, Esther, listen to me! Listen to me, I say! I think there's no doubt that if my wife behaved badly by gossiping to her brother, you behaved equally badly by opening a sealed letter which was quite clearly addressed to someone else."

"She's always writing to her brother, always so sly and so secretive—I never trusted her! And who is she anyway! The illegitimate daughter of a Lancashire rake and some down-at-heel French emigrée who earned her living as a kept mistress."

"I beg your pardon," said Axel, "but I think such remarks about illegitimacy and immorality fall singularly ill from your lips, madam."

"I—" I began, but he said curtly: "Be quiet." And I was.

". . . pretending she's such a lady," Esther was saying furiously, "always trying to behave as if she's so well-bred."

"And so she is, madam, better-bred than you will ever be, for no one who is not ill-bred would ever dream of opening a letter not addressed to them—no, let me finish! Her father was an English gentleman of much the same class as your husband, and I don't think you ever quarreled with *his* birth or breeding. Her mother was a member of one of the oldest houses in France, an aristocrat, madam, far superior to any of your ancestors in rank—you'll pardon me for being so blunt over such a peculiarly delicate subject as rank, but it was after all you who introduced the subject. And as for her illegitimacy, William the Conqueror was a bastard and he was King of England, and besides, the entire Tudor dynasty was descended from the bastard line of John of Gaunt. So let me hear no more talk of my wife being in any way inferior to you, madam, for in fact the reverse is the truth, and I think you know that all too well."

Something seemed to happen to my mind then, the dark hidden corner which I hid even from myself, the raw wound which never closed, the pain which I would never admit existed. Something happened to the nagging feeling that life had been unjust, to the ache of a pride burdened with the weight of inferiority. And something seemed to happen so that I saw this man for the first time, and he was not a stranger to me at all but the man who would stand by me and speak for me and care for me against the world. And all at once the wound was healed and there were no dark corners of the mind which I was afraid to examine and I had my pride and my self-respect restored to me as strong as they ever had been before I knew what the word legitimacy meant. The cure was so vast and so sudden that there were hot tears in my eyes and I could not speak. And I saw him through my tears, and loved him.

Esther was going. She was white-faced, furious still but her fury repulsed, her abuse shattered. Axel had said to her: "Please leave us now," and she had muttered something and turned abruptly to the door, her footsteps brisk and her head held high. After her the door slammed and we were alone.

"Axel," I said, and burst into tears.

He took me in his arms and I clung to him and wept unashamedly against his breast. His fingers stroked my hair, lingered on the nape of my neck.

"Hush," he said at last. "The incident is hardly so tragic as to deserve such grief! It was a greaty pity you wrote such a letter but if Esther feels insulted she has only herself to blame. No matter how much she distrusted you or suspected you of writing such foolishness she had no excuse to open the letter."

I could not tell him I was crying for another reason altogether, but perhaps he guessed for he said: "Her words grated on me. If there's one subject I hate discussing with any Englishman or Englishwoman, it's the subject of class and rank. I've too often been slighted and called a foreigner to have any patience with those who try to invoke their own blind prejudices in the name of social degree." He kissed me lightly on the forehead and while I was still unable to speak he took the opened letter which lay on the secretaire where I had let it fall after snatching it from Esther's hands. "I must say, however, that I do find this letter particularly unfortunate."

It was then at last I remembered what I had written in the letter and the horror flooded back into my mind.

"You read it?" I said, hardly able to breathe. "All of it?"

"Under Esther's direction I glanced at the parts where our names were mentioned." He folded the letter up again and not looking at me put it away in his wallet.

All my old fears and anxieties swept over me again. I felt my limbs become taut and aching.

"May I have the letter, please?" I said unsteadily. "I would still like to send it."

He still refused to look at me. It was the first time I had ever seen him embarrassed. "I'm sorry," he said at last, "but I'm afraid I can't possibly consent to you sending it. I've no wish to censor whatever you may want to discuss with Alexander, but in this case I'm afraid I must."

There was a long silence. I felt the color drain from my face. Finally he brought himself to look at me.

"Much of what you say is—unfortunately—true," he said slowly, "but there is also much that is not true. For example, you assume Mary was poisoned with rat poison kept in the kitchens. I can tell you straight away that Alice does *not* keep rat poison in the kitchens. It was kept there for a time but then a servant girl took some to try and poison her lover, and my father promptly ordered that the poison be made when we needed it and not stored. Also, there's absolutely no evidence that Mary was poisoned. It's true that you can think of a reason why it might have become necessary to murder her, but that's not proof of murder and never will be. Similarly, this is true of all your statements; you say that any of us could have killed my father and that all of us had cause and opportunity, and to some extent this is true, but you have no proof which of us killed him—you haven't even proof that Rodric didn't kill him, and before you can begin to accuse anyone else, I think you should first prove Rodric to be innocent. The only evidence that exists all points to the fact that Rodric killed him, and as for Mary saying she saw Rodric alive after he drowned in the Marsh, I'm afraid I'm still convinced the episode was a figment of her imagination. Anyway, if it's anyone's responsibility to discover who killed my father, it's certainly not yours and I would strongly insist that you go no further with your extremely dangerous inquiries. If Mary was poisoned— and I don't for one moment admit that she was—and there's a murderer in this house, then you yourself would be in danger if you persisted in your foolhardy inquiries. I must insist that you leave the matter alone."

I said nothing. I was too uneasy, too nervous, too full of doubts.

"If you send this letter to Alexander," he said, "you stir up the whole affair anew. He's only a seventeen-year-old schoolboy and young for his years, and God knows what trouble he would cause if he panicked and acted foolishly on the receipt of this letter. Besides, there's absolutely no reason for him to leave school early. He'll be home in three weeks' time for Christmas and you'll see him then."

"Four weeks," I said.

"Three—four weeks—what difference does it make? Things will be better by then. I've no doubt Mary's death has been a considerable shock to you, but by Christmas you'll be feeling much less depressed and will have forgotten this involvement which you mistakenly think you have in my father and Rodric and in the manner in which they met their deaths."

I was again silent. Then suddenly I burst out impulsively: "Need Esther stay at Haraldsdyke?"

"I'll discuss the matter with her."

The silence was uncomfortable. He reached out uncertainly, touched my arm with his fingers. "I'm sorry," he said, "I'm sorry you had to find out about my past relationship with her. I had hoped you would never have to know."

I turned my head aside sharply so he would not see into my eyes.

"It was very brief," he said. "A moment of madness and foolishness for which I've paid very heavily. I had fancied she would now be as ashamed of the memory as I am but apparently she feels no shame at all. I'll see that she doesn't stay a moment longer under this roof than is necessary, but it's possible she may protest or cause difficulties to spite me, so you must be patient if you have to wait a few weeks yet."

"I see," I said.

His fingers pressed against my cheek and turned my face to his. "Whatever I felt for her in the past is quite finished now," he said. "I hope you realize that."

I nodded, not looking at him. "That's why you're so harsh on Ned, isn't it," I said suddenly. "Because he's the only one who knows you and Esther were ever close, and you're ashamed that he knows."

Axel gave a short mirthless laugh. "Ned's a young rogue," he said. "It's probably not his fault, but that doesn't make any difference. There's a certain element of truth in what you say, but I still hold that he's a rascal who needs discipline." He turned aside. "I must go," he said abruptly. "I have to see the rector to make arrangements for the funeral. Vere had gone into Rye to see the undertaker. I'll see you at dinner, my dear, and meanwhile please no more melodramatic letters to Alexander."

He was gone.

Presently I went back very slowly to the bedroom and stood for a moment by the window as I watched the winter sunlight cast a dappled light on the green expanse of the Marsh. Rye and Winchelsea on their twin hillocks seemed deceptively near.

I wanted so much to believe him. I wanted more than anything else now to believe every word he said and not to be tormented so continuously by all my doubts and anxieties. But he had not explained why such a time had elapsed between the descent to the hall to see his father and Esther's screams when she had discovered the body.

He had not let me send the letter to Alexander. And he had refused to admit the possibility that Mary had been murdered . . .

I summoned Marie-Claire, put on a black gown and fidgeted while she dressed my hair. When I was ready at last I went downstairs to the kitchens.

But Axel had been telling the truth about the poison. The cook confirmed the story that no poison had been kept on the premises since the incident with the serving girl.

I went back upstairs to my rooms.

Either Axel was right and Mary had not been murdered at all, or else she had been poisoned. But if she had been poisoned how had the murderer obtained the poison?

I thought of Dame Joan the witch, dismissed the thought and then recalled it, wondering. Dame Joan would know how to prepare a poison. Axel had been in the village that afternoon—he had seen me enter the church . . . He had gone to the village in the hope of finding me, he had said, and had then seen me enter the church. But supposing he had come to the village to get the poison? I had been a long time in the church while I had wrestled with my conscience. Supposing he had seen me go into the church and had then walked past me to Dame Joan's cottage . . .

But I did not really believe Axel was a murderer. It was Axel who understood me. How could I love someone who might be a murderer? But there was no logic any more, only the turbulence of confusion and the agony of doubt. I only knew that love and fear now ran shoulder to shoulder, and that my dilemma seemed even worse than before.

Sitting down once more at the secretaire, I wrote a brief note to Alexander in which without explaining my reasons I begged him to leave Harrow without delay and journey at once to Haraldsdyke.

Ned was in an outhouse by the stables, a gun in his hands. It appeared that he was about to go shooting.

"Will you walk as far as Rye?" I said.

His narrow black eyes looked at me speculatively. He smiled with an air of appraisal. "For you," he said, "I would walk anywhere in England."

"Fiddle-de-dee," I retorted. "I'm not interested in the entire country. I'm only interested in the road from Haraldsdyke to Rye."

"If you're interested in it, then I am too."

"Could you take a letter to Rye for me and see that it goes on the coach to London? You would have to pay for it to be transferred in London to the coach to Harrow in Middlesex. It's for my brother."

"Have you the money?"

I gave him a coin. "This should be enough."

He pocketed it deftly and stowed the letter into the breast of his shirt.

"It's a secret," I said threateningly.

He smiled again. "All right."

"You'll do it for me?"

"I'd never refuse a request from you," he said, and he spoke ironically so that I could not tell how serious he was. "If you ever want anything from me, you know you have only to ask . . ."

The day slipped away. Vere returned from Rye after arranging for the coffin to be made, and Axel returned to the house with the rector who expected to be provided with refreshment. Esther was busy writing to all Mary's distant relatives, and Alice was in conference with the cook to decide on a suitably sombre menu for dinner. It was left to me to interview poor Mary's governess and tell her she could stay at Haraldsdyke for a further month, if necessary, until she found a new position.

This made me remember how nearly I had been forced to be a governess and I spent a long time wondering what would have happened if I had refused Axel's proposal. Perhaps Mary would even be alive . . . but those were useless, abortive thoughts and I did not dwell on them. I did not really want to dwell on any of my thoughts very much, least of all the memory of how I had written again to Alexander against Axel's wishes and had entrusted the letter to Ned.

So I busied myself as much as possible and tried to keep myself fully occupied, and soon it was dark and time for bed.

The next day, Tuesday, followed much the same pattern; several people called to express sympathy and I was busy receiving them courteously and creating a correct impression. The undertakers brought the coffin and Mary was laid out in it amidst the stifling odor of flowers in the small yellow morning room which was normally never used. I went to view the body out of mere respect for convention but I have such a horror of death that I could not bring myself to look in the coffin, and escaped from the room as soon as possible.

The funeral was set for the next day and I retired early to bed to get a good night's rest. I knew in advance that I would find the funeral an ordeal.

In the middle of the night, I woke up suddenly, not knowing what had awakened me, and sat up just in time to see the bedroom door closing as someone slipped out of the room. A glance at the pillows beside me told me that Axel had left. I waited, wondering where he had gone, and then when the minutes passed and there was no sign of him returning I slipped out of bed and donned my woolen wrap.

He was not in the adjoining room. Very cautiously I went out into the passage but it yawned black and empty before me. I nearly went back for a candle, but I thought better of it. I did not want Axel to see me as soon as he came back into sight.

On reaching the landing I glanced down into the hall, but there was no one there either and I was just deciding to go back to bed when I heard the muffled sound of horse's hooves far away. I stood motionless, thinking that I must surely be mistaken, and then I went to the window at the other end of the landing, parted the curtain and peered out into the night.

There was no moon. The night was dark as pitch. Yet I could almost be certain that I heard those muffled hooves again as a horse was ridden away from the house. The minutes passed as I still stood listening by the window, but finally I turned and found my way back to the room. I was amazed. Unless I was much mistaken, Axel had dressed hurriedly, saddled a horse and ridden off into the night.

I lay awake for a long time, but he did not come back. I was just slipping into a drowsy half-consciousness shortly before dawn when I heard the horse's hooves sound faintly again in the distance. I waited, too sleepy to make a second venture down the dark passage to the landing, and at last many minutes later, Axel slipped back into the bedroom and padded through to his dressing room to undress.

When he came to bed he slept straight away as if he were exhausted. His limbs were cold but soon became warmer, as if the night air had chilled him yet the riding had exercised him enough to keep severe cold at bay. I lay awake then, all sleepiness vanished, and wondered where he had been for so long at the dead of night and whether I would ever find out what he had done.

He was very tired the next morning. I saw what an effort it was for him to rise from the bed, and when he was dressed and shaved I noticed the shadows beneath his eyes and the tired set to his mouth. But perhaps the telltale signs of weariness were only clear to me who knew how little sleep he had had, for certainly no one else seemed to notice. Everyone was, in any event, much too preoccupied with the funeral.

Mary was buried that morning in Haraldsford churchyard. Rain was falling. I loathed every moment of the ceremony which reminded me horribly of my parents' death, and the emotional strain together with the fact that I myself had had very little sleep the previous night combined to make me feel exhausted.

But there was no respite, even after the return to Haraldsdyke. Several mourners had to be entertained at a formal dinner, and I had to summon all my reserves of strength to be polite and courteous to some distant cousins of Mary who had traveled from Hastings to be present at the funeral. To my horror they decided to stay the night, and I had to give orders for bedrooms to be cleaned, beds to be aired, fresh linen to be taken from the cupboards.

Before I knew it, it was time for tea to be served and there was no escaping that either. Finally after half an hour of dreariness over the tea cups I managed to retire early to my room where I collapsed before the hearth of the sitting room fire and prayed I would never have to attend another funeral for as long as I lived.

I was still feeling too weary even to make the supreme effort to go to bed, when the door opened and Axel came into the room.

"Aren't you in bed yet?" he said, and there was an edge to his voice as if he found my behavior annoying. "I thought you excused yourself on account of weariness."

"I'm almost too tired to undress," I said, but he wasn't listening and I heard him go through into the other room.

A moment later he reappeared.

"Incidentally," he said, his voice abrupt, "what's this?"

I turned. In his hand was the jar containing Dame Joan's potion which I had hidden so carefully behind the tallboy. As I rose to my feet, the color rushing to my face, I saw the expression in his eyes and realized that he knew exactly what the potion was and what it was for.

We stood there looking at each other, he waiting ironically for me to try to tell lies in explanation, I hating that dreadful day which now seemed to be about to culminate in some appalling scene, and as we stood there I heard the footsteps in the corridor, the light hurried footsteps which I knew and loved, and heard that familiar, much-loved voice shouting my name.

It was as if a miracle had happened. Without a word I ran to the door, flung it open and hurled myself headlong into my brother's arms.

Seven

IT SEEMED THAT Alexander had left Harrow after receiving my first letter hinting that something was wrong, and had not even received my last letter which Ned had taken to Rye for me. He had traveled south as quickly as possible, left his bags in Rye itself and walked from there to Haraldsdyke where Vere had received him in the hall. Vere had been in the process of seeking us in our room to tell me of my brother's arrival when Alexander had pushed past him impulsively, and calling my name had run down the passage as if he feared some mishap had already overtaken me.

"How wonderful to see you again!" I said, tears in my eyes. "How wonderful of you to come!"

Axel was furious. Alexander did not seem to notice that he was not welcomed with enthusiasm by his brother-in-law but I knew the signs all too well, the ex-

treme coolness of voice, the deliberately stilted cour-
teousness of manner, the withdrawn opaque expression in
his eyes.

"Please Axel," I said politely, trying not to sound as
nervous as I felt, "please don't feel obliged to stay up to
receive Alexander. I know how tired you must be."

"On the contrary," he said in a voice so icy I was surprised Alexander did not notice it, "I'm no more tired
than you are. Let me order refreshment for you, Alexander. You must be cold and hungry after your travels."

I saw at once that he had no intention of leaving us
alone together. Frustration mingled with anger overcame
me, but Alexander was saying agreeably: "No, actually I
feel warm after walking, but I'd like some tea all the
same, if that's possible. I'm very partial to tea, particularly in the early morning when it helps me wake up, but
I often drink it in the evening too."

We drank tea. Conversation, smothered by Axel's
presence, drew to a halt. Alexander eventually began to
fidget in the realization that the atmosphere was not as
relaxed as it should have been.

"Perhaps you could show me to my room," he said uneasily to me at last.

"I'll show you," said Axel. "Your sister's had a long,
exhausting day and should have been in bed an hour
ago."

"No, please—"

"But I insist! I'm sorry the room is not particularly
pleasing, but owing to these people staying here overnight
all the best guest rooms are already in use. My dear," he
added to me, "I suggest you ring for your maid and retire
at once."

I did not dare protest. On realizing that it was going to

be impossible for me to see Alexander alone that night, I made up my mind to wait until the morning; Axel could not keep us both under constant surveillance for an indefinite period of time.

Having resigned myself to this, I did not even wait to summon Marie-Claire but hurried to bed as fast as I could so that I could pretend to be sound asleep when Axel returned; I had just closed my eyes when the door of the room opened and he came into the room.

"We'll discuss this further in the morning," he said, ignoring my efforts to appear asleep. "I think it's sufficient to say now that I'm extremely displeased and intend to send Alexander straight back to school to complete his term—if the authorities at Harrow have not already ordered his expulsion for absenting himself without leave."

"But he told us he had permission!" I half-sat up, then lay back again. "He told the housemaster I was ill . . ."

"I have no intention of involving myself in his lies. He leaves Haraldsdyke tomorrow and I shall pay his travel expenses back to Harrow where he must stay for the remainder of the term."

"He won't go!"

"I think he will, my dear. It's I who hold the purse-strings. If he wants to complete his studies at Harrow and then go up to Oxford he will do exactly as I say."

"But I so want to see him—" My voice broke; I was much too tired and upset to keep back my tears.

"And so you will," he said, "at Christmas when he comes here for the holidays."

"I—"

"There's nothing more to be said. Now please go to sleep and rest yourself without prolonging the conversation further."

At least he made no further mention of the potion.

I tried to stay awake so that I might slip out and warn Alexander and talk to him alone, but presently I realized that Axel was waiting till I slept before sleeping himself and I gave up fighting my weariness. Sleep, absolute and dreamless, overcame me and when I awoke the clock hands pointed to eight o'clock and the rain was dashing itself against the pane.

I was alone.

Seizing the opportunity to see Alexander, I did not even pause to dress but merely snatched my wrap as I ran out of the room. Within seconds I was breathlessly opening the door of the smallest guest room which I knew had been assigned to him.

"Alexander," I said. "Alexander!"

He was apparently deeply asleep, sprawled on his stomach on the bed, the right side of his face pressing against the pillow, one arm drooping towards the floor. Beside him was an empty cup of tea. Axel remembered, I thought, surprised and gratified. He remembered Alexander likes tea in the early morning.

"Alexander!" I said, shaking him. "Wake up!"

But he did not. I shook him in disbelief but he only breathed noisily and remained as inert as before. My disbelief sharpened into horror and the horror into panic.

"Alexander!" I cried. "Alexander, Alexander—"

But he would not wake. My arm knocked the tea cup and when I put out a hand to steady it, I found the china was still warm. Someone had brought Alexander a cup of tea as an early morning token of refreshment—and Alexander had awakened and taken the drink.

But now I was unable to wake him.

I was terrified.

I ran sobbing from the room and stumbled back to my apartments in a haze of shock. Finally, in my bedroom once more I pulled myself together with an enormous effort and quickly dressed as best as I could on my own. There was no time to dress my hair. I twisted it up into a knot at the back of my head so as not to appear too disreputable, and then covered my head with a shawl before slipping out of the house by the back stairs to the stables.

But Ned wasn't there. I saw one of the stable-lads.

"Find Mr. Edwin," I ordered him at once. "He may be in the kitchens. Tell him I want to see him."

The boy mumbled a startled "Yes m'm" and scuttled out of sight.

Five long minutes later the back door opened and Ned crossed the yard to the stables. He moved easily with an unhurried gait, oblivious to the squalling rain and the blustery wind of the November morning.

"Good day to you," he said lightly as he came into the stables, and then he saw my expression and his manner changed. "What's the matter?"

"My brother arrived last night," I said unsteadily. "Something's happened to him. He won't wake up and his breathing is odd. Please take me to Rye to fetch a doctor, please—straightway!"

His eyes were wide and dark. "Have you told anyone?"

"I'm too frightened. I must go and get a doctor—please, don't ask any more questions."

"Dr. Salter lives at Winchelsea."

"I don't want the family doctor. Is there a doctor at Rye?"

"There's Dr. Farrell . . . I'm not sure where he lives. Up past St. Mary's, I think . . . let me saddle a horse." And he moved past me swiftly to the stalls.

I leaned back against the wall in relief.

"Someone may well see us," he said when he had finished. "We'll have to ride out down the drive and hope for the best. Will you be able to ride behind me? I'd advise you to ride astride, unless you really object. It'll be safer in case I have to put the horse to the gallop."

"Very well."

He scrambled into the saddle and then almost lifted me up beside him. He was very strong.

"Are you all right?"

"Yes."

We set off. No one appeared to see us. As we went out on to the Marsh road the rain seemed to lessen and the sky seemed lighter in the west. By the time we reached the towering town walls of Rye it had stopped raining and the sun was shining palely on the wet cobbled streets and the dripping eaves of the alleys.

"Listen," said Ned. "I'm not certain where this doctor lives. Let me leave you in the parlor of the George Inn while I go looking for him. I think he lives in the street opposite St. Mary's church, but I'm not sure."

"Very well."

He took me to the George, left the horse with an ostler and ushered me into a room off the parlor. No one was there. We were alone.

"I have money if you need it," I said and gave it to him.

He took the coins and then closed his hand on mine so that I looked up startled.

"There are other ways of repayment than by coin," he said.

I looked at him, not understanding, my whole mind

absorbed with my anxiety, and his face was blurred to me so that I did not even notice the expression in his eyes.

"I'd look after you if you left George," I heard him say. "I'd find work and earn to keep you. I always fancied myself in George's shoes, ever since he brought you home and I saw how young and pretty you were." And suddenly he had pressed strong arms around my waist and was stooping to kiss my mouth and chin and neck. I tried to draw back but his hand took advantage of my movement and slipped from my waist to my breast with an adroitness born of practice.

I twisted with a sharp cry but found myself powerless in the grip of the arm which lingered at my waist. He laughed, his teeth white, his black eyes bright with excitement, and suddenly his greed and his skill and his clever tongue reminded me of his mother Esther and I hated him.

"Bastard!" I spat at him, childish in my helpless fury.

He threw back his head and roared with laughter. "The pot calls the kettle black!" he exclaimed, and drew me all the closer so that he could force his wet mouth on mine and make his hamfisted fingers familiar in places where they did not belong.

I froze in revulsion.

The next thing I knew was the draft of an open door, a gasp rasping in Ned's throat as his muscles jerked in shock, the sudden removal of all offense. I opened my eyes.

Axel was on the threshold. His face was white and dead and without expression, but the opaque quality was gone from his eyes and so was all hint of their withdrawn look which I knew so well. His eyes blazed. His hands were tight white fists at his sides. He was breathing very rapidly.

"So I was not quite in time," he said.

Ned was backing away against the wall. "George, she asked me to take her to Rye to find a doctor—"

"Get out."

"—her brother's ill—"

"Get out before I kill you."

Ned moved unsteadily towards the door without another word. I could see Axel trying to restrain himself from hitting him and the effort was so immense that the sweat stood out on his forehead. And then as Ned tried to shuffle past him, Axel seemed to find self-control impossible. I saw him seize Ned by the shoulders, shake him and then hit him twice with the palm of his hand before slinging him out into the corridor.

The door closed.

We were alone. I suddenly found I was trembling so violently that I had to sit down.

All he said was: "I told you not to come to Rye with Ned."

And when I did not reply he said: "I think you're too young to have any idea of the power you have to rouse a man's deeper feelings. I suppose you have no idea that Ned wanted you from the moment he set eyes on you. You were too young, your eyes were blind. Your eyes are probably even blind now as you look at me. You're far too young, you're incapable of understanding."

I dimly realized he was trying to excuse my behavior. I managed to stammer: "I only thought of Alexander . . . I knew Ned would take me to Rye—"

"Alexander," he said, "is not in danger. One of the stablelads has gone to Winchelsea for Dr. Salter."

"I wanted another doctor—"

"Dr. Salter is perfectly reputable."

"But Alexander—"

"Alexander," said Axel, "appears to have taken a non-fatal dose of laudanum. Are you ready to go?"

"Yes, but—"

"Then I suggest we leave without delay."

I followed him mutely to the courtyard where he had left his horse.

"But how—" I stammered, but he would not let me finish.

"I don't propose to discuss the matter here," he said curtly. "We can discuss it later."

But even when we arrived back at Haraldsdyke he still refused to discuss the matter.

"I'm taking you to your room," he said to me, "and you will stay there for the rest of the day. I am becoming tired of watching you to make sure you do nothing fool-ish, and your behavior has been so far from exemplary that I don't think you can say I'm not justified in insist-ing you remain in your room today."

"But Alexander—"

"Alexander will get better without any help from you. He can stay on a few more days here and then you can talk to him as much as you like, but you may not talk to him today."

"But—" I began and then Vere came to meet us and I had to stop.

"My wife has been very upset by her brother's illness," said Axel abruptly to Vere. "She wants only to rest all day. Please ask Alice to make arrangements with the ser-vants not to disturb her—she'll be sleeping in our room and I shall move into Rodric's old room so that she may have the maximum amount of peace and rest without interruption."

I was too embarrassed by this open reference to the fact that we were to have separate rooms, to take notice of Vere's reply.

Upstairs I moved towards the corridor which led to our rooms, but he put his hand on my arm and guided me instead down another corridor.

"I've changed my mind," he said quietly. "You shall stay in Rodric's room. I'll bring you anything you may need."

I looked at him in amazement. "But why can't I stay in our rooms?"

"I've changed my mind," was all he said. "I'm sorry."

"But—"

"Please!" he said, and I saw he was becoming angry. "You've flouted my wishes so often recently that I must insist that you don't attempt to disobey me now." He opened the door of Rodric's room and gestured that I should enter. "I'll come and see you every few hours to see you have everything you need," he said abruptly. "Meanwhile I advise you to lie down and rest. And if anyone comes to the door, don't on any account answer them. Do you understand?"

"Yes, Axel."

"Very well, then. I'll return to you in about an hour's time." And closing the door without further delay I heard him turn the key in the lock before walking away swiftly down the echoing corridor.

The mist rolled over the Marsh and smothered the house with soft smooth fingers. The silence seemed to intensify as the hours passed, and it seemed at last to me as

I waited in Rodric's room and watched the dusk fall that the silence was so absolute that it was almost audible. Axel had come twice to the room to see if there was anything I had needed, but he had not stayed long and by the time the dusk began to blur with the mist it was a long time since I had last seen him. I stood up restlessly and went over to the window to stare out into the mist, my fingers touching the carving on Rodric's huge desk, and I thought of Mary again, remembering how she had admired Rodric and how we had spoken of him in this room.

The hours crawled by until I could no longer estimate what time it was. The increasing boredom of the enforced confinement made me irritated, and I was just wondering in a fever of impatience how late it was when I heard footsteps outside in the corridor and Axel came in with a tray of food.

"How are you?" he asked peremptorily, and added: "I'm sorry I was so long delayed in bringing you some food. I intended to bring it earlier."

"It doesn't matter—I haven't felt hungry." I wanted to ask a multitude of questions, but I guessed instinctively that he would refuse to answer them. "Axel—"

"Yes?" He paused on his way out of the room, his fingers on the door handle.

"When may I leave this room?"

"Tomorrow," he said, "but not before then."

"And Alexander—"

"He's still drowsy and is resting in his room. He'll be well enough tomorrow. You needn't worry about him."

The door closed; his footsteps receded. I sat down on the edge of the bed again without touching the food and drink on the tray, and tried to be patient and resigned, but I found the inactivity hard to endure and after a while began to rearrange the contents of the desk drawers in an agony of restlessness.

I heard the footsteps much later, when I was contemplating undressing and trying to sleep. The floorboard creaked above me and made me look up. Presently it creaked again. After listening intently I thought I could distinguish the muffled tread of footsteps as if someone was pacing up and down the room above my head.

But there was nothing above this room except the attics and no one slept there any more.

I took the candle and went to the door but the lock was firm and there was no breaking it. I looked around in despair, and then for the third time searched the drawers of the desk, but there was no duplicate key conveniently waiting to be discovered. My glance fell on the knife which lay on my dinner tray. Seizing it I went back to the door, inserted the blade between the door and the frame and scraped at the lock.

Nothing happened.

I stepped back a pace and stared at the door in frustration. Then I took the candle, and holding it at an advantageous angle I peered into the eye of the lock. It was difficult to be certain, but I thought the key was on the other side and that Axel had not troubled to remove it altogether.

Going back to the desk I took two sheets of notepaper from the drawer and inserted them under the door side by side with one another. Then I took the fork and poked it into the keyhole.

The key fell to the ground without much trouble. Holding my breath I stooped and carefully pulled the sheets of paper back through the gap between the floor and the bottom of the door, and soon I saw that the key had fortunately not bounced off the paper on falling to the floor; it came gently towards me on the notepaper, and a second later I was turning the lock to set myself free.

As I opened the door it occurred to me that the footsteps overhead had stopped some minutes before, but I did not pause to question why this had happened. I tip-toed very quietly down the passage, my hand on the wall to guide me, the candle snuffed and abandoned in the room I had just left so that I was in darkness.

The house seemed still enough, but as I neared the landing I could see the light shining from the hall and heard the soft murmur of voices from the drawing room nearby. I hesitated, fearful that someone should come out of the drawing room as I was passing the door, but I knew no other way to the back stairs, so at last I took a deep breath and tip-toed quickly across the landing to another passage at the far end.

Nobody saw me. I paused, heart beating fast, and listened. Everywhere was quiet. Moving into the shadows once more I found the back stairs to the attics and cautiously began to mount them one by one.

I was convinced that the footsteps I had overheard above Rodric's room had been Alexander's, and had immediately suspected Axel of imprisoning him in the attics for some reason. Who else would be pacing up and down there as if he were a caged animal? And into my memory flashed the picture of the diamond-cut inscription of Rodric's on the attic windowpane, the reference to his own imprisonment there as a boy. That room at least had been used as a prison before, and if my guess of the house was correct, tonight it was being used as a prison again.

I reached the top of the stairs, and paused to get my bearings. Nervousness and excitement made me clumsy. With my next step forward my ankle turned and I stumbled against the wall with a loud thud. I waited, my heart in my mouth, my ears straining to hear the slightest sound, and once I did think that I heard a door opening and closing far away, but nothing further happened and in the end I judged the noise to be my imagination.

It was pitch dark. I wished desperately that I had brought my candle, for I wasn't even sure of the way to Rodric's attic. At last, moving very quietly, I felt my way down the passage until I reached the point where the passage turned at right angles to run into another wing. I was just beginning to be unnerved by the total blackness when I turned a corner and saw a thin strip of light below the door at the far end of the corridor. I edged towards it, the palms of my hands slipping against the cool walls, my breathing shaky and uneven.

The silence was immense. The prisoner had evidently not resumed his pacing up and down. Some quality in the silence unnerved me. Would Alexander ever have submitted so silently to imprisonment? I visualized him breaking down the door in his rage or shouting to be released, not merely sitting and waiting in passive resignation.

I started to remember ghost stories. My scalp prickled. Panic edged stealthily down my spine, but I pulled myself together and stepped out firmly towards the light which was now not more than a few paces away. It would never do to let my nerve weaken now.

I was just stretching out my arm to guide me alongside the wall when my fingers encountered a human hand.

I tried to scream. My lungs shrieked for air, the terror clutched at my throat, but no sound came. And then a hand was pressed against my mouth and a voice whispered in my ear: "Not a sound, whoever you are" and the next moment the door nearby was pushed open and I was bundled into the dim candlelight beyond.

The door closed. I swung around, trembling from head to toe, and then gaped in disbelief.

My captor gaped too but presently managed to say weakly: "Mrs. Brandson! Why, I do beg your pardon—"

It was young Mr. Charles Sherman, the bachelor brother of James Sherman, the lawyer of Rye.

"Good heavens!" I said still staring at him, and sat down abruptly on a disused stool nearby.

"Good heavens indeed," said Mr. Charles, smiling at me uncertainly as we recovered from our mutual shock. "I wonder if you are more surprised than I or if I am more surprised than you?"

"You could not possibly be more surprised than I," I retorted. "Forgive me if I sound inhospitable, but may I ask what on earth you're doing hiding in the attic of Haraldsdyke at the dead of night, sir?"

"Dear me," said Mr. Charles, torn between his obvious desire to explain his presence and his equally obvious air of conspiratorial secrecy. "Dear me." He scratched his head anxiously and looked puzzled.

This was not very informative. "I suppose it's some sort of plot," I said, since it clearly took a plot to explain Mr. Charles' encampment in the attic. "Did my husband bring you here? What are you waiting for? How long do you intend to remain?"

Mr. Charles cleared his throat, took out a handsome watch from his waistcoat pocket and glanced at it hopefully. "Your husband should be here in a few minutes, Mrs. Brandson. If you would be so obliging as to wait until he arrives, I'm sure he will be able to explain the entire situation very easily."

I was quite sure Axel would do nothing of the kind. He would be too angry that I had escaped from Rodric's room to indulge me with long explanations of his mysterious activities.

"Mr. Sherman," I said persuasively, "could you not at least give me a little hint about why you should be pacing the floor of this attic tonight and waiting for my husband? Please! I know a woman's curiosity is her worst and most disagreeable feature, but—"

"Ah, come, come, Mrs. Brandson!"

"There! I can tell how you despise me for it, but—"

"Not in the least, I—"

"—but I'm so worried about my husband, and if you could just help to put my mind at rest—oh, Mr. Sherman, I would be so grateful to you—"

I had fluttered my eyelashes enough. Mr. Charles' natural kind-heartedness and fondness for flaunted femininity had made him decide to capitulate.

"Let me explain from the beginning, Mrs. Brandson," he said graciously, and sat down on the edge of a table opposite me for all the world as if we were pausing in some drawing room to pass the time of day. "I am, as you so rightly assumed, here at your husband's bidding in an attempt to prove once and for all beyond all reasonable doubt who killed Robert Brandson last Christmas Eve.

Your husband has known from the beginning that Rodric could not have killed his father, but for reasons of his own he was reluctant to speak out at the time. For various reasons of delicacy I cannot elaborate further on this except to say that your husband saw Robert Brandson alive and well *after* Rodric had quarreled with his father and ridden off over the Marsh. Therefore he knew Rodric could not have been responsible for Robert Brandson's subsequent murder . . ."

Esther, I was thinking, Esther. Robert Brandson must have caught Axel with her in her rooms. After the quarrel with Rodric he must have gone upstairs to talk to his wife and found Axel with her—in her bedroom . . .

". . . let me explain what happened: according to your husband, on the day of the murder," Charles Sherman was saying, "your husband took Rodric out shooting on the Marsh since Rodric and Vere had come to blows and George thought it would be best to separate them for a while. When they came back Robert Brandson called to Rodric from the library and summoned him inside to see him."

"Because he suspected Rodric of being involved in smuggling and in league with Delancey."

"Precisely. Rodric told your husband afterwards—"

"But they didn't see each other afterwards!"

"Oh yes, they did, Mrs. Brandson! Patience, and I shall explain it all to you. Rodric told your husband afterwards that this accusation was untrue but that when he had tried to deny it to his father and cast the blame on Vere, the conversation had abruptly degenerated into a quarrel. Rodric walked out and rode off on to the Marsh and Robert Brandson, in a great rage no doubt, stormed upstairs to discuss the matter with—"

Esther, I thought.

"—your husband George—"

Esther, I thought again, and Axel was there. Robert Brandson wanted to ask his wife if she knew which of their two sons was guilty of smuggling and conspiring with Delancey.

"—but George could not help him. However, shortly afterwards he decided to go down to the library to discuss the matter further with his father—"

To talk his way out of a compromising situation, I thought, and to beg his father's forgiveness.

"—and it was then," said Charles Sherman gravely, "that he found Robert Brandson dead. His immediate reaction—after the natural grief and shock, that is—was one of horror in case he himself, or indeed someone else whom he knew to be innocent—"

Esther.

"—was suspected of the crime. He hesitated for some minutes, trying to decide what to do, and then Esther—pardon my informality, I mean Mrs. Brandson—arrived on the scene—"

Liar, I thought. She was with Axel all along, conferring with him, trying to decide what to do.

"—and her screams roused the servants and the other occupants of the house. Rodric was naturally suspected, but Esther refused to believe it, since Rodric was her favorite son, and to pacify her George rode off after Rodric with the idea of warning him and sending him into hiding until there was proof of the murderer's true identity. As I've already said, George himself thought Rodric must be innocent but was prevented from saying why for reasons of delicacy."

"Quite," I said.

Mr. Charles looked at me uneasily and then quickly looked away. "Well," he said, clearing his throat again, "your husband did in fact catch up with Rodric and tell him that someone had killed Robert Brandson and that all the evidence pointed to the fact that Rodric had murdered him. Rodric was all for returning to Haraldsdyke and confronting the person he suspected of murder, but George begged him to be more prudent and eventually Rodric appeared to acquiesce and agree to go into hiding. George suggested they should make a faked death for Rodric for two reasons. First because Rodric would find it easier to flee the country if everyone thought him beneath the Marsh, and second because his mother wouldn't have the same compulsion to clear his name—and thus perhaps jeopardize her own safety—as she would if he were alive and in exile. George said he knew it was a cruel thing to do, but he reasoned he was doing it as much for her own good as for Rodric's; Mrs. Brandson had long been estranged from her husband, you know, and this would have given her a motive of sorts for his murder; if suspicion were diverted from Rodric it might well have fallen upon her.

"George told Rodric to travel to Vienna and go to his house there for food and lodging. George said he would return to Vienna and meet him there as soon as the inquest was over, and fact he did leave Haraldsdyke as soon as decency permitted and hurried overseas once more, even though Haraldsdyke was now officially his, subject to the one contingency he later fulfilled by marrying you. Robert Brandson, suspecting Rodric of being in league with Delancey and Vere of being incompetent in handling money, had evidently decided to entrust his wealth to your husband.

"Now when George returned to Vienna, Rodric wasn't there. He searched high and low for him, had inquiries made and so on, but he couldn't gather together any evidence that Rodric had even left England. Naturally this made George very suspicious—especially when he remembered how Mary Moore, poor child, had come to him before he had left England with a wild story of seeing Rodric at Haraldsdyke after Rodric's official *death* in the Marsh. George had dismissed the story at the time, but now he began to wonder. Supposing Rodric had changed his mind after they had parted, walked back to Haraldsdyke leaving his horse and hat by the mere as evidence of his death, slipped into the house by the back stairs and gone to the rooms of the person he suspected of murder in order to confront that person with the truth. And supposing that person had managed to kill him, hide the body and later bury it in secret so as not to disturb the convenient story of Rodric's accidental death in the Marsh as he was guiltily fleeing from the scene of the crime—"

"But Mr. Sherman," I said, interrupting, "who is this person whom Rodric—and now my husband—suspect of Robert Brandson's murder?"

He looked at me as if surprised I had not already guessed, and made a gesture with his hands. "Who else but your brother-in-law Vere?"

The candle flickered in the dark as a draft breathed from the casement frame, but the silence was absolute. I stared at Charles Sherman.

"George suspected Vere from the beginning," he was saying. "As soon as he returned to England he began to search for evidence and two days ago he found it and rode that same night to Rye to ask for my help. We agreed Vere must be guilty, and worked on a plan to trap him once and for all. We reasoned that Vere had cause enough to kill his father—since his father was threatening to go to the Watch at Rye, Vere's whole future and livelihood were at stake. It was vital to him that his father should be silenced. Also Vere had the means and the opportunity to poison Mary, he knows about poisons which kill weeds in the soil and improve the agricultural qualities of the land, he probably has a stock of such poison somewhere on the estate. He could have tampered with the tea Mary drank—George tells me it was Vere who carried the tray upstairs from the hall."

"True . . . So you and my husband are planning . . ."

"What we hope will be a successful trap. We arranged that I should ride over here at dusk today and Axel would meet me at the gate and smuggle me up the back stairs to this attic where he would show me the evidence he had uncovered. We realized we would have to wait till after the funeral before putting our plan into action, as everyone would be too busy on the day of the funeral itself, but then at last when the funeral was over, who should arrive at Haraldsdyke but your brother Alexander! It at once seemed as if everything was doomed to failure, for George knew that if Alexander were once to speak to you alone, you would tell him every detail of the suspicions you had outlined in your long ill-fated letter which was never posted. Then Alexander would be sure to create havoc by making some unpleasant scene. George knew that he himself only needed another twenty-four hours grace, and he was quite determined that no one should interfere with his plans at that late stage. It was easy enough to keep you apart till morning, but when morning came George knew he had to act. In desperation he took some of Mrs. Brandson's laudanum, went down to the kitchens and ordered tea. When it was ready he took the cup from the kitchens, put in the laudanum and gave it to the footman to take to your brother's room."

"And then I panicked," I said dryly, "And not without cause."

"No indeed," Mr. Charles agreed. "Not without cause . . . But before George followed you to Rye he left that same ill-fated letter of yours to your brother in the library where he knew that Vere would be sure to find it; apparently Vere usually goes to the library to write any correspondence connected with the estate or else to read the newspaper in the hour before dinner. When George brought you home, he told me he was careful to tell Vere to inform Alice that you would be sleeping alone in your apartments tonight. Then after putting you for your own safety in Rodric's old room, he returned to the library— and found the letter had been moved slightly and the hair he had placed on it had fallen to the floor. So it was plain Vere had seen it. We were almost sure that on reading the letter Vere would decide that you knew too much for his peace of mind; in particular you knew about Vere's past involvement with Delancey, and this you remember, was *not* common knowledge. It was supposed that Rodric, not Vere, was the smuggler and the traitor. We thought Vere would try and kill you and put the blame on your husband. According to George himself, one of the servants saw you ride off with young Ned to Rye this morning—it would soon be common knowledge within minutes, and everyone knows Ned's reputation. Later they would think your husband had killed you in a rage."

My eyes widened. "You mean—"

"But of course," said Mr. Charles, "You're not sleeping alone in your room, as Vere supposes. You're safe here in the attic with me, even though your husband intended that you should be safely behind the door of Rodric's room."

But I was not listening. There were footsteps in the corridor, light muffled footsteps, and the next moment the door was opening and Axel himself was entering the room.

I stood up, covered with confusion, and sought feverishly in my mind for an explanation. Axel saw me, turned pale with shock and then white with rage, but before he could speak Charles Sherman intervened on my behalf.

"George, I regret to say I'm to blame for this for your wife heard me and came upstairs to investigate. I thought it best to tell her a little about the situation so that she could assist us by being as discreet and silent as possible. I feared that if I kept her in ignorance she would have had a perfect right to complain very loudly indeed at my somewhat clandestine presence in her household."

Axel was much too adroit to ask me angry questions or to censure me in the presence of a stranger. I saw his face assume a tight controlled expression before he glanced away and pushed back his hair as if such a slight gesture could release some of his pent-up fury.

"I apologize for leaving the room, Axel," I said nervously, "but I thought the footsteps I overheard belonged to Alexander and I decided—wrongly, I know—to try to talk to him."

"It's unfortunate," he said without looking at me, "but now you're here there's little I can do to alter or amend the situation." He turned to Charles Sherman. "Everything is ready and everyone has gone to their rooms. We should take up our positions without delay."

"Which positions do you suggest?"

"If you will, I'd like you to go to my apartments. You can hide yourself in the dressing room on the other side of the bedroom beyond the bed. I'll be at the head of the stairs and will follow him into the bedroom and block his exit into the sitting room should he try to escape. We'll have him on both sides then."

"By God, George, I hope your plan succeeds. Supposing he didn't in fact read the letter? Or supposing he read it and decided not to act upon it in the way we anticipate?"

"He must," said Axel bluntly. "He's killed three times, twice to protect the original crime from being attributed to him. He won't stop now. Let's waste no more time."

"No indeed, we'd better go at once."

Axel turned to me. "It seems I dare not trust you out of my sight," he said dryly. "You'd better come with me."

In the doorway Mr. Charles stopped, appalled. "Surely, George," he began, but was interrupted.

"I would rather have my wife where I can see her," said Axel, still refusing to look at me, "than to run the risk of her wandering about the house on her own and spoiling all our careful plans."

I said nothing. I was much too humiliated to argue, and I knew his lack of trust was justified.

"And remember," he said quietly to me as Mr. Charles went out into the corridor, "you must be absolutely silent and do exactly as I say. I don't know how much Charles told you, but—"

"Everything, within the limits of what he termed 'delicacy.'"

"Then you'll understand how vital it is that nothing should interfere with our attempts to set a trap. I presume I may trust you not to scream no matter what happens."

I promised meekly to make no noise under any circumstances.

We set off down the passage then, and as Axel carried a single candle, its light shaded with his hand, I was able to see the way without trouble. At the top of the back stairs, however, he extinguished the flame and put down the candlestick on the floor.

"Follow me closely," he whispered. "We're going to the landing. If you're frightened of not being able to keep up with me or losing me in the dark, hold the tails of my coat and don't let go."

I smiled, but of course he could not see my smile for we were in total darkness. We started off down the stairs, my left hand on the bannisters, my right holding one of his coattails as he had suggested, and presently we stood in the passage below. When we reached the landing a moment later it seemed lighter, probably because there were more windows in the hall than up in the attics, and I was able to make out dim shapes and corners. Axel led me to the long window on one side of the landing and we stepped behind the immense drawn curtains.

We waited there a long time. I felt myself begin to sway slightly on my feet.

Beside me Axel stiffened. "Are you going to faint?"

I looked coldly through the darkness to the oval blur of his face. "I never faint."

In truth I was shivering and swaying from excitement,

nervousness and dread rather than from the arduousness
of standing still for so long. I leaned back against the
window to attempt to regain my composure, and then just
as I was standing up straight at last I again felt Axel stiff-
en beside me. Following his glance I peered through the
small gap in the curtains before us.

My limbs seemed to freeze.

A shape, muffled in some long pale garment, had
emerged noiselessly from the dark passage and was crossing the landing to the stairs. Presently it reached the hall
and disappeared. From far away came the faint click of a
door opening and closing.

I wondered where it had gone, but dared not speak for
fear of breaking that immense silence. We went on waiting. And then at last the door opened far away and closed
again and the next moment the pale shape emerged into
the hall and came silently up the stairs towards us.

I might have been carved out of stone. My limbs were
quite still and the only moving organ in my body was my
heart which seemed to be banging against my lungs with
an alarming intensity. I was aware only of thinking: this
is a murderer walking to meet his victim. And; I am the
person he intends to kill.

The figure reached the landing. There was nothing then
except the shallowness of our breaths as we waited motionless by the slightly parted curtains. A moment later
the shape had passed us and had begun to move down the
corridor towards our rooms. It carried a gun, one of the
guns used for shooting game, a gun such as the one which
had killed Robert Brandson.

"Follow me," Axel's order was hardly louder than an
unspoken thought. "But not a sound."

He moved forward noiselessly.

The door of our apartments was open. I saw a flicker of white enter the bedroom and for a moment to obscure the light of the single lamp burning by the window. Someone seemed to be asleep in the bed, but the light was uncertain, a mere dim glow from the table several feet away. And then as I watched, the figure in white raised the butt of the gun and began to bludgeon the shapeless form in the bed.

My hand flew to my mouth, but even as I stood still in horror I saw the door of the dressing room open slowly, and as Axel reached the threshold Charles Sherman stepped out to stand opposite him across the room.

The white figure with the gun ceased the bludgeoning, having no doubt realized as suddenly as I did that the figure in the bed was an illusion, a clever trap.

There was a moment when time ceased and the scene became a tableau. Then at last:

"So it was you who killed my father, Alice," said Axel, appalled.

She did not scream.

All I remember now is the great stillness, the silence as if the whole house were suffocated by the shrouds of the mist outside. Even when Alice dropped the gun and began to move, she made no noise but seemed rather to glide across the floor, her white robe floating with an eerie grace so that it seemed for one bizarre moment that she was a ghost, a mere evil spirit seen on Hallowe'en. The gun fell softly onto the bed and made no sound.

Both men stepped forward simultaneously, but Alice was too quick for them; as I watched I saw her hand flash out towards the dresser, grasp a small phial which stood forgotten among the ornaments and wrench off the cap with a quick twist of her strong fingers before raising the phial to her lips.

It was the potion Dame Joan had given me, the potion overlooked by both Axel and myself in the distraction of Alexander's arrival the night before.

Alice drank every drop. Even as Axel shouted her name and sprang forward to stop her she had flung the empty phial in the grate, and after that there was nothing any of us could do except stare at her in shocked disbelief as she smiled back into our eyes, then the poison gripped her like a vice and she fell screaming towards the death which she had first intended for me. I had never heard a human being give such screams or twist her body into such contorted shapes. I stood watching, transfixed with horror, unable to move; and then suddenly all the world heeled over into a bottomless chasm and I did not have to watch her any more.

For the first time in my life I fainted.

Eight

"SHE SUBSTITUTED THAT potion, of course," said Axel. "Dame Joan wouldn't have given you poison without Alice egging her on, and Alice did not even know you intended to see her mother that day. But later when her mother told her about the potion Alice must have seen a chance to dispose of you and so she substituted a jar of poison. Then when you apparently ignored the potion and remained alive she must have decided to club you to death by force—especially after she had heard the contents of the confiscated letter you wrote to Alexander and knew you believed Mary and were convinced Rodric was innocent of the crime. You were a great danger—not so much to her, but to Vere who was a more obvious suspect. So you had to be killed, quickly, before you could make any further attempts to display your suspicions to the world."

It was on the afternoon of the next day. We were in our own private sitting room and outside beyond the window a pale November sun was shining across the sweeping expanse of the Marsh. Downstairs Alice was laid out in the horrible yellow morning room where Mary had lain before her burial, and Vere was still shut in the room with his wife as if his poor grieving presence could somehow bring her back to him from beyond the grave.

"I ought to have realized that Alice, not Vere, was the murderer," I said. "If your father was killed because he was threatening to expose Vere's association with Delancey's smuggling, Vere could hardly have killed him because he didn't know his father had found out the truth. When I overheard that conversation between Vere and Alice it was Alice, not Vere, who knew that Rodric had denied being involved with Delancey and had accused Vere of being the guilty one, and Alice who knew that Mr. Brandson more than half believed Rodric despite his earlier conviction that Rodric was guilty. I suppose that after Alice dragged Mary out of the saloon and pretended to go to the nursery to see the children, she must have slipped back to the saloon to eavesdrop on the entire quarrel. Then she would have realized that to save Vere from serious trouble she would have to kill Mr. Brandson before he could act on his supicions, and then would have to try to make a scapegoat of Rodric."

"She succeeded very well in some respects," Axel observed wryly. "Rodric had left his gun in the library after the quarrel; the weapon—the perfect weapon for involving Rodric—was waiting for her as soon as she herself entered the library. When Rodric left, my father went upstairs to talk to Esther to discover how much she knew, and while he was gone Alice must have entered the library from the saloon, picked up the gun and waited for him to return. Perhaps she waited behind the door and struck him as he came into the room . . . I suppose it was this use of force that made me think of the act as a man's crime. I never stopped to consider that Alice with her broad shoulders and strong arms was physically quite capable of committing the murder."

I was piecing together the remaining fragments of information in my mind. "Ned must have come into the hall from the stables soon after that," I reflected. "He told me he knocked on the library door and received no reply. By that time Mary would already have returned to the drawing room after running after Rodric to the stables . . . Esther was upstairs in her apartments, and—" I stopped, blushed, looked away.

"—and my father found me with her when he stormed upstairs to see her after his quarrel with Rodric." I sensed he too was looking away. He was standing very still, as if absorbed with the pain of memory. "I've never felt so ashamed in all my life," he said after a pause. "It certainly served to bring me to my senses with a jolt, but then even before I could begin to apologize to my father and beg his forgiveness he was murdered."

The bitterness and regret in his voice was unmistakable. In an effort to turn to some other aspect of the situation I said in a rush: "Axel, what *did* happen to Rodric? I suppose Alice really must have killed him?"

"Yes, of course she did. I would assume he returned to the house—strictly against my advice, of course, but then he always was reckless—to confront Vere, whom he suspected, and try to force the truth out of him. He probably went to Vere's apartments but found not Vere, as he had hoped, but Alice, who was unable to resist the temptation

to kill him to preserve the fiction that Rodric was a murderer who had met his just end in the Marsh. After all,
how much more convenient to have a corpse for a scapegoat than a live protesting innocent man! I presume she
caught him unawares and stunned him; he did not suspect
her, remember, and so wouldn't have been anticipating
such a thing."

"But what did she do with his body?"

"I wondered about that for a long time. In the end I
made a thorough search of the attics and found a leather
bag which I had often seen Alice use to take presents
from Haraldsford to her mother. I wondered why Alice
no longer used it, and then on examining it I saw that the
interior was bloodstained. After searching the attic further
I found an old meat cleaver from the kitchens under a
loose board in the floor and I began to grasp what had
happened. Even then I still didn't think that Alice had
dismembered the body and taken it piece by piece to be
buried in her mother's patch of land at Haraldsford; I
suppose I didn't think a woman could be capable of such
a gruesome task. I merely thought Vere had found the
discarded bag in the attic and used it to convey the dismembered body to some remote section of the Marsh.
When I showed the cleaver and bag to Charles Sherman
yesterday it didn't occur to him either that anyone but
Vere could have been responsible. But we underestimated
Alice."

"So Rodric's body . . ." I recoiled from the idea.

"It may not be buried in Dame Joan's herb patch, but I
shall most certainly suggest to the authorities that they
look there before assuming the body to be buried in the
Marsh. No matter how many journeys Alice made to her
mother's cottage, her visits would never have given rise to

suspicion. What more natural than that she should call on her mother? It would have been the easiest way for her."

I shuddered.

"Of course Alice was also responsible for Mary's death, I think there can be no doubt of that. It seems reasonable to assume that she obtained a phial of poison from her mother whom she visited with the child after church that morning, and then later put the contents of the phial in Mary's cup of tea. I should have remembered that it was Alice who suggested having tea after dinner, and it was Alice who left the room in person to order the tea, ostensibly to spare the servants on a Sunday but in reality no doubt to get the phial from her room. And I should have remembered too that it was Alice who poured out the tea when it arrived. But I didn't remember. I was too busy suspecting Vere."

"I wonder if Vere read my letter which you left in the library to trap him," I said. "I suppose he did read it and then went straight to tell Alice and to ask what he should do."

"He must have done," Axel agreed, "for Alice was a country girl—she could barely read and could only write the most elementary words which she needed in maintaining the household accounts."

"Then perhaps Vere did realize that she was guilty— perhaps they agreed together that I should be killed."

"No, I'm certain Vere wasn't involved to that extent. I've talked to him, and I'm convinced of his innocence. Alice never made him an accomplice because she was too busy trying to protect him: from my father, from Rodric, from Mary, and finally from you." He stood up and moved over to the window to stare out over the Marsh before adding abruptly: "I didn't think you'd be in any danger at all when I brought you to Haraldsdyke." He was facing me again, moving back towards me. "I still think you wouldn't have been in any danger if you had been accustomed to behaving as a conventional young girl might be expected to behave, but since you have this remarkable talent for seeking all possible danger and running headlong towards it—"

I laughed at this. "No, Axel, that's not fair! I was only puzzled and curious."

"You were also a constant source of anxiety to me, my dear," he retorted. "However, be that as it may . . . by the way, how exactly did you manage to escape from that locked room? When I found you in the attic with Charles Sherman, I very nearly killed you myself out of sheer exasperation!"

I described my escape meekly.

"You amaze me," he said, and he was not angry any more, I noticed to my relief, only amused. "I can see I shall never be able to place you safely under lock and key again."

"I hope," I said, "that the need to do so will never arise."

He laughed, caressed my cheek with his finger and leaned forward to brush my lips with his own.

"Am I forgiven for my multitude of deceptions and evasions and, I very much fear, for frightening you on more than one occasion?"

"You leave me no alternative," I said demurely, determined to make him endure the pangs of conscience for as long as possible. "Besides, why didn't you trust me?"

"Did you trust me?" he said, and he was serious now, the amusement gone. "Wasn't I merely a stranger to you? Didn't you consider yourself merely bound to me by ties born of convenience? Can you honestly tell me you loved me enough to merit a confidence of such magnitude?"

I could not look at him. I fingered his hand which rested on mine and stared down at the carpet. "Did you expect me to love you straight away?" I said painfully. "You didn't love me. I was a mere child to you. And still seem so, no doubt."

His hand covered mine now and closed upon it. "Your only childishness lies in your lack of perception," he said. "If you were older you would have perceived all too clearly that from the beginning I found you exceedingly attractive. However, I tried to hold myself apart from you as often as possible because I sensed from your questions before our marriage that you disliked the idea of extreme intimacy. It was, after all, a marriage of convenience, and although you were benefiting to a certain extent by consenting to it, I was certainly benefiting just as much from your consent and I wanted to make things as pleasant for you as possible, at least for a time."

I remembered my tears at Claybury Park, my loneliness and distress.

"I merely thought you didn't care."

"I cared more than I would ever have dreamed possible," he said, "and soon came to care even more than that. When I found you with Ned at Rye, I knew I cared more than I had ever cared for anyone in my life before. The bitter part—the ironic part—was that having for the first time in my life experienced this depth of emotion, I found it increasingly evident that you were not attracted to me. I seemed to fancy you looked too long and often at Ned, and then there was that business of the potion—"

I was consumed with shame. My cheeks seemed to be afire. "Did you see me leave Dame Joan's cottage?"

"Yes, and knew at once why you had gone there."

I stared miserably down at his hand clasped tightly in mine.

"My dear, if you really feel—"

"I feel nothing," I said rapidly, wanting only to repair the harm I had done. "It's all past now—I never want to see another potion again."

He was silent, wondering, I suppose, if this meant that I cared a little or was merely recoiling from the sordidness of the incident and my narrow escape from death by poisoning.

"It was only because I was frightened," I said. "Frightened of you, frightened of the unknown, frightened of the world. But that's all gone now. I'm not frightened any more."

He was silent still, but his hand relaxed a little. I looked up and saw his withdrawn expression and longed to smooth it from his eyes.

"I wish we could go away," I said impulsively. "I wish we didn't have to stay here. I'm sure I shall never sleep soundly in our bedroom again for fear of seeing Alice's ghost. And the house is so gloomy and oppressive when winter closes in and the mist thickens over the Marsh. I hate it."

"I hate it too," he said frankly to my astonishment. "I always did. I never intended to stay here long—the only reason for my return was to clear Rodric's name and bring my father's murderer to justice. After that I intended to give up the estate by deed of gift to Vere's son Stephen and appoint Vere and the Sherman brothers trustees until the boy comes of age. That will mean Vere can live and work on the estate he loves while the Shermans can curb his more extravagant tendencies. And Vere will be happy in the knowledge that the estate will belong to his son and heir outright. I thought that was the best solution."

"Oh yes indeed!" I tried not to sound too pleased. Stifling my immense relief at the prospect of escape from Haraldsdyke and life in the country I added hesitantly: "But where will we ourselves go? What is to happen to us?"

He smiled at me and I saw he knew what I was thinking. "I've come to the conclusion," he said softly, "that you're much too beautiful to be incarcerated in the depths of the country where no one can see you. I think I'll take you to my town house in Vienna, my dear, to the city I love best in all the world, and you shall make a sparkling, glittering entrance into Viennese grand society."

"Well, that's all very well," said Alexander plaintively when I told him the news later, "but what about me? I shan't be able to come and visit you in the holidays."

"You'll only be at school for a little longer," I pointed out, "and after that you shall come and visit us in Vienna."

"But Vienna . . . well, I mean, it's rather foreign territory, isn't it? Are you sure you'll be all right?"

"But we're as foreign as Axel!" I reminded him crossly. "You always forget that half our inheritance comes from across the Channel. Besides, if Axel wanted to go to America, I would go with him. I would travel around the world with him, if he decided to go."

Alexander looked at me wonderingly. "You're so strange," he said with a sigh. "I shall never be able to keep up with you. You'll be telling me next that you're in love with him . . ."

Vere was grateful to Axel for granting Haraldsdyke to Stephen, but he remained numbed by his loss for a long time, and for at least ten years after Alice's death our rare visits to Haraldsdyke were gloomy, depressing occasions indeed. However, he did eventually remarry when he was about thirty-five years old, and after that the atmosphere at Haraldsdyke became more normal and welcoming to the casual visitor. His second wife was a nice woman, a widow a few years his senior whose first husband had been a clerk in some legal firm in Winchelsea; Vere evidently preferred women of an inferior rank to himself, although his second wife was socially far superior to Alice. Of Vere's three children, Stephen lived to marry and perpetuate the family name, but his younger brother died of diphtheria in childhood, and his sister, although living long enough to marry, died in childbirth a year after her wedding. On the whole I thought that branch of the family more inclined to misfortune than any of the others.

As for Ned, he went to America, became immensely rich, but never married. We heard news of him from Vere to whom he wrote regularly, and twice he came back to England for a visit, but of course we were in Vienna and never saw him.

Esther married that most eligible bachelor Charles Sherman and thereafter lived at Rye, which presumably suited her better than her life as Robert Brandson's estranged wife at Haraldsdyke. But I suspect not much better. Esther was not the kind of woman born to be contented.

Rodric's bones were exhumed from Dame Joan's herb

patch and given a proper Christian burial at Haraldsford church. Dame Joan herself denied all knowledge of Rodric's death, but naturally no one believed her. I suppose it might have been possible to charge her with being an accessory after the fact of murder, but I was superstitiously reluctant to meddle with her and so, I discovered, was everyone else. The villagers of Haraldsford summoned the courage to mass before her door and threaten to burn down her cottage, but she dispersed them with a wave of her broomstick; they all turned tail and fled for fear of being cursed and irrevocably doomed. Shortly after that incident Vere sent out a warning that anyone who did not leave her well alone would have to answer to the justices of the peace for his conduct, and Dame Joan was abandoned with much relief to her customary solitude.

My one sorrow during the years that followed my arrival in Vienna was that although he wrote often enough Alexander never visited us; he had decided to pursue a political career, and as it did not pay in the English political arena to have foreign connections, my brother spent much time concealing his French blood and Austrian relatives. However, in the end this availed him little, for the English have no more love for bastards without respectable pedigrees than they have for foreigners, and Alexander's background ultimately told against him. After that, much disillusioned, he went out to the colonies and settled in Jamaica where he managed to involve himself profitably in the spice trade. I thought of him sometimes, far away in a home I had never seen, but on the whole as the years passed I did not think of him too often. I was too absorbed in my own family, my own life.

After we had been in Vienna several years, Axel inherited both a title and more property there from a distant cousin, and the acquisition of the title opened for us all the doors into every section of Austrian society, even those saloons which had previously been beyond our reach. Vienna was ours; and what now can be written about the Vienna of today, the most glittering city in all Europe, which has not already been written? Vienna spiraled to a brilliant zenith of romantic grandeur, and I was there when those sweeping beautiful tunes with their hidden sadness and sensuous nostalgia first enchanted the world. For the waltzes more than anything else seemed to symbolize the new era unfolding in that ancient unique city, and the new era was my era and I was there when it began.

But still sometimes when I sleep I dream not of the brilliant ballrooms of Vienna but of another land of long ago, the land of the green Marsh and of the cobbled alleys of Rye, and suddenly I am on the road to Haraldsdyke again and dreading the moment when I must set foot once more within those oppressive walls. But even as I finally catch a glimpse of the house in my dreams, the mist creeps in across the Marsh with its long white fingers, and I know then that I shall never again reach the Haraldsdyke of my memories, and that it has disappeared forever behind the shrouded walls of time.